Second Act

The Backlot Series - Book 1

Kimberly Page

*This is for all the ladies (and gents) who've always wanted to take a (second) chance on their dreams.
You still can.*

author's note

Dear Reader,

Welcome to the land of fiction! While the events in this book are entirely fictional, they're inspired by the very real shifts happening in the entertainment industry today. From streaming services to increased conversations around diversity, Hollywood is changing—and a lot of that change is motivated by you, the consumer, the fan. Your voice matters.

More than ever, there's an opportunity for audiences to see themselves on-screen in authentic ways. It's something I'm passionate about, and while I'm no expert, I've done my best to reflect some of the issues I've seen over the years.

As a reader, fan, and viewer, you have the power to influence this industry. Your movie tickets, streaming subscriptions, downloads, and yes, even the books you choose, send a message to creatives about what you want to see. It might feel like the big studios aren't listening, but trust me—they are.

I hope you enjoy this peek behind the curtain into the

world of entertainment, and that it leaves you thinking about how we can all help shape the stories being told.

P.S. If this book was rated by the Motion Picture Association (MPA), it would get at least an NC-17 rating for strong language, use of alcohol, and sexual content. The doors are open in Blair's and Wyatt's bedroom scenes, folks.

Somebody That I Used To Know - Gotye, Kimbra

ocean eyes - Billie Eilish

Wait - Maroon 5

The Man - Taylor Swift

Still into You - Paramore

Never Really Over - Katy Perry

So High School - Taylor Swift

Back To You - Selena Gomez

Love Of My Life - Harry Styles

Photograph - Cody Fry

You Belong With Me (Taylor's Version) - Taylor Swift

What We Had - Sody

Run the World (Girls) - Beyoncé

Bad Liar - Selena Gomez

Falling - Harry Styles

How You Get The Girl (Taylor's Version) - Taylor Swift

I Like Me Better - Lauv

golden hour - JVKE

One and Only - Adele

Forever - Noah Kahan

one

. . .

BLAIR

"WHO'S THE HOTTIE?"

My assistant Stella leans over my shoulder to get a closer look at my searched images of Sophia Ford, the twenty-four-year-old best actress Oscar winner, and her brother. Sophia is on my list of dream clients to represent. With any luck, I'll convince her to sign with me before summer's over. However, her brother should have received an Oscar for his role as the popular guy in high school who can make you believe anything he wants.

"His name is Wyatt Bradford, and he's not that hot."

He is that hot.

Dark blond hair, short on the sides and a little longer on the top, but in this pic, it's slicked back. His eyes gaze into the camera and are the same ice blue I remember. Still tall and still working out, I see. That shirt is struggling to stay buttoned across his toned chest. His tan suit wraps around his body, hugging his muscular thighs, and is that a crease right there, or is that...

"Ohmygod, Blair, you can see the outline of his penis!" Stella shrieks behind me.

I slam the laptop closed, stand, and walk away from the desk to get a breath of clean, Wyatt-free air and shake his memory out of my head. I haven't spoken to Wyatt in twelve years. He looks good. Exactly like a selfish dick who would lead you on and then stomp all over your heart. But still undeniably hot.

"Were you able to get passes for the *Pink Slip* season two premiere?" I ask Stella as I grab my phone. She follows me out of my office as we head down to the conference room for our team huddle.

I discovered that Sophia is obsessed with the dark comedy about managers killing off employees who aren't meeting their potential in the office. I've seen a few episodes. It reminds me of a *Hunger Games* meets *The Office* mashup. It's dark but funny.

"Of course I did." She gives me a disappointed look for daring to doubt her. "I'll have a courier bring them to her tomorrow. You still want to go, too, right? And will you have a plus-one?"

I see the look of hope in Stella's eyes, always rooting for me and my "one day it will happen" plus-one. I both love and hate that she's a hopeless romantic.

"Just me."

"Well, I've got something better than a plus-one for you. Sophia agreed to meet with you. She's shooting at Everest Studios this week and can meet between her scenes."

"The greatest thing I've ever done in my life was hire you," I say while going in for a hug.

Stella started interning for me during her senior year of college, and I hired her as soon as she graduated. It's been three years now, and we've been inseparable ever since. She's my secret weapon, and some days, I think she knows me better than I know myself.

"Oh, stop it, Blair. I hate it when you get dramatic about things that are literally in my job description." She blushes, but I know she loves the praise.

As one of the top female talent agents in this city, I have a reputation as a girl's girl. I was in law school during the #metoo movement and had a front-row seat to the shift for women. The opportunities I had to impact and support legislature during law school were historical. Too bad I only realized I didn't want to be a lawyer after I graduated.

So, I moved to LA, and in a moment of right place, right time, I met Lance Wynn. He's the CEO of The Wynn Agency—a talent agency known around Hollywood as TWA. He seduced me with the idea that I could make a difference. As an agent, I could find and sell stories that might change the world, stories that might shed light on topics like poverty, discrimination, or injustice. Plus, my background and law degree would give me a leg up in the negotiation and contract process. Lance sold me when he grabbed my hands across the bistro table we were sitting at for lunch and told me he believed women were the future of this industry.

That was my first lesson about how this town works. Tell your client whatever they want to hear to close the deal. I do focus on women—I almost exclusively sign female talent—but getting Lance to take any of my projects seriously, or prioritize them, is getting harder. After the pandemic, it's like the

Hollywood mindset has reverted to "the good old days," and the scramble to make money has the industry leaning on the tried-and-true superheroes and sequels.

But I'm determined to prove the future is female. That's the reason for the Sophia Google search. Her current agent is an icon in the industry, and she's old school. Rumor has it she's retiring this fall and Sophia's looking for someone who can capitalize on her recent accolades and prevent her from being cast in stereotypical roles.

I want to represent her. I know I would be a perfect fit for her.

If Sophia agreed to meet, then it's my opportunity to lose. She wouldn't entertain the conversation if she weren't open to the idea of representation. I have some leads on a few significant projects I know she will be interested in, and I know I can convince her I'm the right choice. The premiere this week will help spotlight some of my contacts and relationships, too.

"Fine. But you know it's true." I take a seat at the large conference room table while Stella joins the other assistants in the chairs along the wall. The assistants are the lifeblood of this agency, but God forbid they get a seat at the table.

When I open my laptop, the image of Wyatt is still on the screen. The search took me right down the rabbit hole to Wyatt's bio. He works for his father's law firm, which isn't a surprise, but he had other dreams.

As general counsel, Wyatt guides the firm's attorneys on a wide range of matters, including client intake, legal ethics and professional responsibility, engagement management, and policy development and compliance.

Wyatt earned his Juris Doctor from the UCLA School of Law, where he served as an editor of the UCLA Law Review. He graduated magna cum laude from the University of California, Los Angeles, with a bachelor's degree in political science and a minor in accounting.

My investigative skills must be lacking because I could only find his bio on the law firm's website. It doesn't tell me anything about if he's single or dating or what he's been doing for the last twelve years. Would it kill him to get an Instagram account? I'd even settle for a Linked In account.

"Ok, please tell me we've booked Timmy to host the *SNL* season finale," Lance says, diving right in as he pushes through the door and sits at the head of the table.

"Done. And we've booked Olivia as the musical guest, too," says Brian, another agent and Lance's pet.

Lance looks up from his phone as a grin stretches across his face. "That's what I'm talking about. Teamwork makes the dream work."

It takes all my physical control not to roll my eyes.

"When does shooting begin on *Speed* 3?" I ask. "I may need Sandy for an appearance."

"In two weeks. Just let me know, and I'll see if we can make it work." Brian leans back in his chair, feeling cocky and comfortable. Another sequel for the win.

"Blair, what about Michelle? Were you able to lock her

into the lead for *Aquaman 3*?" Lance directs his question to me, but his attention is on the phone in his hand.

"Almost done. There's also a lead opportunity for her in Elizabeth's next untitled project." Yep. That gets his eyes up.

"Instead of focusing on projects that aren't a priority, perhaps you could focus on signing talent?" Lance stands and walks out before I can respond, and I take a sip of my coffee to regulate the rage bubbling under the surface.

"Ignore him," Stella says.

"Easier said than done." I grab my phone and coffee, and rise from my seat.

Stella is infringing on my personal space before I reach the exit of the conference room. "So, you gonna tell me the backstory on Wyatt?" She wiggles her eyebrows up and down, smiling at me.

I pick up my pace back to my office, trying to avoid this conversation. "I'd rather not," I mumble. Why does it feel like I can't breathe?

I'm quiet for a beat too long.

"Oh, my God–is he an ex? Did you sleep with him?" Her hands fly up to her cheeks.

I told you she knows me.

"It's ancient history."

"When? I know everyone you've dated." She puts her first and middle fingers of both hands up to air quote "dated."

"It's nothing. We went to high school together. I haven't seen him since." I play it off like it's no big deal, but my heart feels like it's being squeezed between Wyatt's metaphorical hands to remind me I'm still not over the hurt.

I've dated casually, been married—and divorced—and

had no trouble recovering and moving on with my life. But one mention of Wyatt Bradford has unlocked the secret compartment of emotions I buried a long time ago.

"Do you know Sophia, too?" Stella asks.

"I don't. Well, not really. I knew Wyatt had a little sister, but she was a lot younger than us. She dropped part of her last name, so I didn't put it together immediately." I think back to one of the few times I met Sophia. Her father signed her up for a junior golf camp at the country club where I worked. She joined her father and Wyatt for lunch that week, and I was their server. I doubt she would even recall the interaction.

"He probably doesn't even remember me." I sift through the files on my desk to signal the end of this conversation. Thankfully, Stella catches on quick and just smiles before she turns to go back to her desk.

"Actually, Stella? Cancel the courier and set the meeting with Sophia for tomorrow if you can. I'll hand deliver the *Pink Slip* passes. It'll be a great icebreaker to start the conversation."

There's no reason the topic of her brother should even come up, so we can keep it buried where it belongs until I've proven I'm the right agent for her.

two

. . .

WYATT

"SON! COME IN HERE FOR A SECOND."

I almost made it past him. My father is in the large conference room overlooking downtown LA, sitting in a white leather club chair surrounded by lights and cameras for his weekly *LawTalk* video web series. When in Hollywood, I suppose.

"Hey. What's the topic today?" I ask, feigning interest as I cross the room to see what he wants.

"Just a little update on California's new employment laws. You sure you don't want to join me for this?" It's the last thing on earth I want to do, especially with him.

"Can't today. Meeting Soph for lunch," I say. "Did you need something else?"

"Send her my love." He seems relieved at my rejection as he settles back into his hosting pose. "We have a new client coming in on Thursday, and I'll need you there. I'll send the details over." With a wave, I'm dismissed. He doesn't wait for questions because he doesn't allow them.

Jackson Bradford has spoken, and now the conversation is over.

My grandfather started Bradford and Associates, but my father has turned it into one of the most elite law firms in the U.S. We employ over three hundred lawyers and have offices in six locations. We support a variety of sectors, but we primarily focus on mergers and acquisitions, corporate reorganizations, and shareholder activism.

Even though it's clear my future is to continue the success he's created and eventually lead the company, my father still expects me to earn partner. Too bad it's the last thing I want.

I make it down the stairs and out the door with no other interruptions and jump in the Town Car waiting for me. I haven't seen Sophia in a few weeks. She's been busy enjoying the perks of being an Oscar winner while also filming a guest-star spot on a new series for one of the streamers.

I'm so proud of her. She started acting in school plays as soon as she was able and pushed my parents to let her audition for a kids' network open call. When she landed the lead role for a new series at age twelve, it shocked all of us, but at the same time it didn't surprise us either. She was born to be in front of a camera.

There's no traffic as we wind down the side streets to Everest Studios, and I relax, knowing we'll make it there on time. She wanted to meet today because she's looking for a new agent and needs my advice. Dad and I work with a lot of the talent agencies in town, and I have some insight into the pros and cons of each one. I don't know many talent agents directly, though.

Except one.

Blair Barton. Actually, it's Bennett now. I can't believe she married someone. I used to believe that we would get married. Funny how things change. And how incredibly wrong I was.

The phone vibrates in my hand, bringing me back to the present.

SOPHIA

Almost here?

ME

Yep. What's craft services serving today?

SOPHIA

Something delicious I'm sure.

Sophia may be tiny, but she eats like a man trying to put on game-day weight. I have no idea where she puts it all.

ME

Everest catering never disappoints.

ME

Be there in 20. Love you.

SOPHIA

My phone buzzes again, and I'm expecting to see Sophia's name, but it's an email from my best friend, Jake. It's the itinerary for our annual Manmorial Weekend in San Diego—a weekend with a shit-ton of golf, whiskey, and debauchery. I look forward to it every year, but it looks like this year, Jake will be a little tame because he's engaged. He's been planning his wedding since we were in college, way before he ever had a hint of a fiancé. Jake just loves love. I shoot off a text to fuck with him a little.

> **ME**
> Is your mom joining us in La Jolla?

> **JAKE**
> What? Why would my mom be going?

> **ME**
> Oh, so she just created our itinerary then?

> **JAKE**
> Fuck you. You know I can't go to some places we typically go to.

> **ME**
> Right. You're in love. Or whatever…

I flinch, hoping I haven't reopened old wounds. I can't stand his fiancée, and Jake knows exactly how I feel. While he understands she's not for everyone, he's completely in love with her. I care deeply for Jake, and because he loves her, I do what any best friend would do—I support him the best I can.

> **JAKE**
> You should try it. Maybe someone would finally sleep with you.

> **ME**
> Hilarious.

> **JAKE**
> Where are you? Wanna grab lunch at Joan's?

ME

> On my way to have lunch with Soph—raincheck?

JAKE

> Tell Soph hi…

Jake was my roommate throughout undergrad and law school. He's one of the top entertainment lawyers in LA and close to making partner at Hays and Cole, one of the best entertainment law firms in town. It's where I'd love to work and where I will never get to work. Bradford and Associates is my legacy. The minute I was born, my destiny was preordained.

As much shit as I give Jake, I get it. It must be an incredible feeling to fall in love and build a life with someone. I just don't think it's in the cards for me. I've tried. I even lived with a girl during the pandemic. However, I hate flings and one-night stands even more. Luckily, I have a few arrangements in place when the need arises.

Speak of the devil.

BETHANY

> Hey love, I'm in town this week if you have time for dinner.

ME

> Can I let you know? New client starting.

BETHANY

> Of course. If it can't work, I'll be back in a few weeks.

I run my hand through my hair and catch my reflection in the rearview mirror.

What am I doing?

I should lock in time with Bethany right now. A new client won't keep me that busy. But I'm not feeling it lately. I'm in a funk. Maybe it's because Jake is getting married and I'm losing my wingman. Not that he's been a wingman for a while now.

Or maybe it's because I already had my chance at love twelve years ago. When I watched it fail spectacularly, I knew nothing else would even compare to what we had.

three

. . .

BLAIR

ON MY RIDE to Everest Studios, I scroll through pics and interviews with Sophia to make sure I know all I can about her. I know she makes her living pretending to be someone she's not, but she looks incredibly happy and well adjusted for someone who started in this town at such a young age.

She's already won an Oscar—she's incredibly talented—and her movie won Best Picture because audiences want—no, crave—movies that push you to think and feel. Women make you think and feel. Just as much as any man can.

The unwritten rules in Hollywood are so deeply embedded that it's hard to break the carefully crafted mold, especially if you are a woman. But I continue to watch the trends in our industry, and the old guard is acutely unaware of the power a woman-led, woman-produced, or woman-directed story can have on a box office or ratings. Just tuck it into the "consistently underrated" file.

I've witnessed Reese Witherspoon build a lucrative empire by elevating women's stories. I'm in awe of her ability to consistently prove the value of women in front of and behind the camera, often amplifying diverse voices. She's inspired a dream of mine to open my own talent agency focused on representing marginalized talent, primarily women.

I take one more look at my file on Sophia. I've done my homework, and I know in my heart she is of like mind in this space. As I step into her makeup trailer, I see a tall, dark, and handsome man with his fingers smudging gloss across Sophia's lips.

Holy hotness.

"Hello, gorgeous," a young Ricky Martin look-a-like says to me. "Welcome. Come on in."

"Am I interrupting?" I ask. "I can wait outside."

I didn't mean to interrupt an intimate moment between Sophia and whoever this handsome stranger is. Go, Sophia! I didn't realize she was dating anyone.

Sophia turns in her chair. "Blair?"

"Yes, that's me!"

"I'm so excited to meet you! Brandon, this is the agent I was just telling you about."

I'm immediately nervous. I shouldn't be. I've closed deals with some of the biggest stars out there.

"I think I'm more excited to meet you!" I confess. "I hate to admit it, but I'm a little nervous!"

"Ha, nervous. Nobody's ever been nervous around a five-foot-nothing woman in Hollywood."

I laugh at the joke, even though it's laced with so much truth.

She's flawless in real life. And tiny. Her dark hair forces

you to notice her ice-blue eyes. The same eyes as Wyatt, although that seems to be the only similar feature.

"Hi, Blair. I'm Brandon. And you're not interrupting."

"Oh, no, not at all," Sophia says. "Brandon is a stunt actor and doing a few scenes with me today. He's one of my best friends. We met when I started in the business. He has a problem with personal space and filters, so please excuse him in advance."

"Nice to meet you, Brandon." I reach out to shake his hand, and just as Sophia warned, he knocks it away and comes in for a big bear hug.

"Here, take my seat," he says.

As I settle, Sophia immediately makes me feel welcome and comfortable. She asks me questions about myself and what it's like to work for TWA. I tell her a little about my client list and projects, and I tease a few that I know are coming. I keep it strictly professional but feel a little guilty that I don't even mention that I know her brother. Wyatt has nothing to do with this, though, and I don't want to win—or lose—this opportunity based on a past connection with him. I decide right then to keep the past where it belongs. I'll wait until I've established credibility on my own and there's a better time to bring it up casually.

She admits that her agent is retiring and she is looking for new representation. I listen as she gets right into it.

"I want to parlay this Oscar win into more meaty roles. I want to Kate Winslet the shiitake out of my career."

I smile at her use of the word shiitake. I've heard she doesn't swear. Years of kids' programming will likely do that to you.

"I hear you have a reputation for finding powerful roles for women," she says.

I beam at the compliment while flinching on the inside. I can find her great roles. I can find her roles that women have written and women are directing. My concern is that Lance will try to leverage her star power for traditional and male-led blockbuster opportunities. Not that she shouldn't do that. It's just getting harder to influence him these days.

"I know I'm still considered new in this business," Sophia continues, "but I've been here for years, and I'm ready to move into more than just acting. I want to produce and eventually direct."

I nod as she talks. This is fairly normal for actors.

"I was so lucky to have Edna as an agent. She took me in and treated me like family. I trust her more than my family sometimes!"

I should confess right now that I know her brother.

"Edna is amazing," I say. "One of the real people in Hollywood. She's been a mentor and role model for me as well. And I completely get it. I'm tired of watching the seventh sequel to another action franchise or another remake of a nineties hit when there are so many fresh stories and storytellers out there. And so many of them are women."

"That's why I was dying to meet you." She turns back to me and takes my hands in hers.

"Ok, ladies. I'm due on set." Brandon looks up from his phone. "I'll let you two talk about your plans for women to take over the world, and I'll see you after lunch," he tells Sophia as he leans in to kiss her cheek.

"Don't be a hater, Brandon!" Sophia teases with a playful slap on his arm.

"You know I'm not. My sisters made sure of that. I grew up and live in a world ruled by women. It's been a fantastic life!" He winks as he heads toward the exit.

Right as he opens the door, I hear a voice I'll never forget call out, "Who's hungry?"

I turn and see the gorgeous man I've been stalking on the internet in the name of research. I freeze. I must look like a deer in headlights. I watch as Wyatt Bradford steps inside the room with that charming smile and slight dimple on his left cheek, completely oblivious to what he's just walked into.

He scans the room, and the moment his gaze lands on me, recognition erupts on his face. "Blair?"

I look back at Sophia and can see the look of surprise and confusion on her face.

"You know Wyatt?" Sophia says.

Yes, Sophia. Yes. I know him better than I'd like to admit.

four

. . .

WYATT

SHE LOOKS INCREDIBLE. I guess I should have expected that, but it's been twelve years since I've seen her. At least in person. I do my best to take a casual look up and down without it being creepy.

"Yes, Wyatt and I went to high school together." Sophie looks back and forth between us, still surprised. "He dated my best friend, Holly."

Blair is responding to Sophia, but her eyes are locked on mine. And yes, I dated her friend Holly, but there's a little more to the story than she's sharing.

"I remember Holly! She was so nice to me. And so pretty, too. What happened to her?" Sophia asks. "I don't think you've had a proper girlfriend since."

Ouch. Unfortunately, Sophia doesn't realize what a wound she's just opened.

"What did happen to Holly? We lost touch after graduation," Blair spits out with an edge to her voice.

That stings.

"What a coincidence. We did, too," I bite back.

I watch as she slowly rises and walks my way, and my heart threatens to explode out of my chest. She raises her arms and wraps them around my neck, leaning in to hug me.

"It's nice to see you again," she says.

I can feel her breath on my neck, and chills run down my arms. I realize my hands are still hanging at my side, and I move quickly to wrap her in an embrace. She feels so good against me. Her hair still smells like citrus and vanilla. I don't realize that my eyes are closed and I'm leaning my cheek on the top of her head until I feel her pull away.

"Yeah, you, too."

I'm flooded with unfamiliar emotions, feelings I thought I'd gotten over long ago, but obviously, I've just buried them. I'm pulled between longing to be in her orbit again—where we can hide away from the world and tell each other our dreams—and resentment and shame. Blair knew my deepest secrets, but she's also the only person who saw what a coward and fraud I really am.

I became close friends with Blair during sophomore year. She was a server at the country club where I played golf. I would spend my weekends hanging out in the restaurant, waiting for her to take a break so we could talk. Her best friend, Holly, started hanging out with us toward the end of the year, and the three of us were inseparable. But Holly showed more interest in me, so we started dating our junior year. Blair seemed more interested in being friends back then, so I thought little of it.

Halfway through our senior year, Holly and I fizzled out,

and I started spending more time with Blair. And it felt like we were becoming more than friends.

She was the only person I confided in about the scout from Stanford who came to see me after I won at the American Junior Golf Association Invitational. My father was supportive of athletics, but it took a backseat to academics. He'd already arranged for me to attend UCLA—his alma mater—and follow in his footsteps. After that win, my coaches urged me to explore playing in college, even suggesting I could have a career in the sport.

Blair encouraged me to apply to Stanford and helped me put together the application and a reel of my tournament play to submit with it.

But I fucked it all up. My dad found out and lost his mind. It was then that I realized he was supportive because golf was another skill that would benefit me in my law career. A great way to network. He blamed Blair, said that I'd lost my way. I didn't stand up to him, and we basically stopped hanging out. I left for UCLA without saying goodbye, and she never called me. And that was the end of it.

"This is like a mini-reunion!" Sophia says. "You're welcome for reconnecting the two of you."

Blair's chin drops to her chest, and I can see her close her eyes for a beat. She turns to face Sophia and flashes a smile, but I can tell it's fake. It doesn't reach her eyes.

"I'm sorry I didn't tell you I knew Wyatt. I didn't want to seem like I might take advantage of a connection to meet you. But I can see how it might look like I was hiding something, too."

I can see Sophia trying to digest all this new information.

She's been burned before, and her eyes dart my way for some reassurance.

"Blair would never take advantage of you, Soph. She's the real deal," I tell her.

Blair looks at me with surprise and what looks like maybe a little anger, but I'm not exactly sure why that would make her mad.

An intern knocks on the trailer door and breaks the tension.

"Sounds like they need you for a quick script change," I say. "Blair and I can catch up while we wait."

"Ok," Sophia replies, "but don't go anywhere. I'm starving."

I turn to face Blair after Sophia leaves.

"I'm just going to run over to the commissary and get some fresh air," Brandon says. "It's way too hot in here for me." He wipes his lips seductively.

Jesus. I thought he left already.

"I should go, too," Blair says.

"Wait."

She hesitates, waiting for me to say something, but my mind goes blank. I rake my hand through my hair and then shove it in my pocket. Blair is gorgeous. She always has been, but this is a grown-up version with fuller lips, thicker hair, and honey-colored eyes filled with confidence. Every feature is amplified, as if in high definition. When we met, she had a look of wholesome innocence. She wore little makeup and was constantly wearing athletic shorts and tank tops, with her hair pulled up and off her face. And she was always eating ice cream. Which brings me back to those lips. Maybe they are the same lips. I loved those lips.

"What, Wyatt?" Blair says, snapping me out of my memories.

"Do you still like ice cream?" I ask. A look of confusion crosses her face. "It's just that you always ate ice cream. Even if it was freezing out," I laugh. "I just wondered if you still do."

Blair doesn't respond. Instead, she breathes in deeply and lets out a slow sigh.

"I know this is weird, but let's just keep this as professional as possible. I really want to represent Sophia. I think we'd do a lot of great things together. That's all I want. Let's keep the past in the past."

Blair has effectively shifted right back into agent mode. I stay quiet.

"Maybe you could look at the materials I sent to Sophia," Blair continues. "It appears she values your advice. You know this town as well as I do, and it's not who you know but who knows you. And the only thing people know about Sophia is she had one good movie and is beautiful."

"She's got an Oscar," I say defensively. "That means something around here."

Blair bends down to grab her purse. "She does, but fifteen minutes can go fast in this town if you can't convert. Then that Oscar will only get her on a highlight reel in future shows."

I watch her walk toward the door, knowing that she's right.

"I'll see you tomorrow?" I ask.

"Why would I see you tomorrow?" She looks confused.

"I'm Sophia's plus-one for the *Pink Slip* premiere. I assume you're going?" I hold my breath while I wait for her to respond. If she says yes, I hope Sophia hasn't already asked someone else to join her. I had managed to keep Blair out of sight and out of mind for so long. But now that I've seen her again, I can't go back to pretending she doesn't exist.

five

. . .

BLAIR

I THINK I'm having a panic attack. I can't believe he showed up here. And why the fuck did he ask me about ice cream? I knew he would be here. Don't ask me how. The minute Stella caught me obsessing over his pics and set up a meeting with Sophia, something in my gut told me he was nearby.

He's taller, over six feet now. And the man knows how to wear a suit. His face has matured, but those eyes. I mentally bite my fist. His eyes are framed with the darkest lashes I've ever seen. I used to be jealous of those lashes.

I'm pacing in the parking lot, eyes shifting to Sophia's trailer because I'm terrified Wyatt may walk out and see me. I pull out my phone and immediately FaceTime my best friend, Jess, hoping she's not in some meeting. I need to see her now.

"Hey, babe. What's up? You ok?"

Praise be. She answered.

"Um, hey. So, do you remember me talking about Wyatt in college?" I ask.

"Wyatt. Let me think. Was he the hot lay that got away?"

"Something like that," I mumble. "I just saw him. He's Sophia Ford's brother."

"Shut the fuck up." I see her prop her phone up somewhere on her desk, and then she grabs her laptop and starts typing to find more info on him.

Jess is a reporter and podcaster for one of the hottest subscription entertainment pubs, and she's been my best friend since college. She's LA-born and bred and looks the part, too. Golden tan skin, light brown hair that morphs into golden blonde from spending so much time in the sun. Perfect skin with just a whisper of freckles–enough to disguise any blemish, assuming she even gets blemishes. She barely wears makeup but always looks runway ready. When *The Beach Boys* sang *California Girls* they were talking about her. We met when she approached me in line at freshman orientation and asked to see my schedule. She's incredibly nosy and has built the perfect career around her thirst to know everything about everybody all the time. It's a sickness, really.

She knows the complete story about Wyatt. How crushed I was when he started dating Holly because I thought he and I had connected instantly. How we finally got together after he and Holly broke up. How he took my virginity and then ripped my heart out when he got back together with Holly shortly after we slept together.

She also had a front-row seat while I did my best to get over it—by getting under another guy—in college. It didn't go well, but Jess insists the guy was just supposed to be a rebound and nothing more. I tried to date a few others, but at best, it would end in more of a one-night-stand situation, and at worst, I wouldn't make it past the first five minutes without finding an excuse to ditch. Maybe my standards were too high, but I never felt the tingles people talked about—like the flips my stomach made every time I saw Wyatt.

"He wasn't wearing a ring," I say, "and he looks even better than I remember."

I don't have to say anything else. She stops typing and stares at me for a minute, her mouth slightly open. One thing I love about Jess is her ability to read minds—and that she knows me well enough to know I'm totally freaking out.

"I'll meet you at my apartment in fifteen minutes," she says.

Jess hands me a glass of chardonnay the minute I walk in the door. I love coming to her place because it's full of color and has the feeling of a soft landing. I head straight for the cloud couch and sink in while Jess heads back to the kitchen to grab some popcorn and Twizzlers.

"So, I made a few calls," Jess says. "The headline is never been married and definitely single. At least nothing that would be considered a relationship."

"His sister said he hasn't had a girlfriend since high school."

"Interesting. He works for his father, too," she says.

"I know."

"How do you know?"

"When I was prepping for Sophia, I saw some photos of them together. I went down the rabbit hole," I confess.

"My sources tell me he's well respected and very influential."

"That tracks. I would expect nothing less than perfect for Wyatt Bradford." I can't help the bitterness coming out. Wyatt was my first love—in every sense of the meaning—and I foolishly thought he would be my only love. I can't believe how wrong I was about him. It was silly of me to think that all the time we spent together meant something. Instead, he was just playing the long game to get into my pants. He basically used me for sex and then got right back together with Holly— my best friend, although, by that time, we weren't really friends anymore.

Wyatt never promised me anything, but we talked about staying close after we graduated. Even though I was headed to Boston College, I thought about applying to Stanford or maybe even UCLA. If I couldn't get in for my freshman year, maybe I could at least transfer by sophomore year.

I was destroyed the summer after graduation and the whole first semester of college. Thank God for Jess. I wouldn't have made it without her.

"You going to be ok?" Jess breaks me out of my zoned-out state, and I tell her I'll be fine.

"So, not to add to the shit pile, but your ex will be on the red carpet tomorrow night."

When it rains, it pours. My ex is Billy Bennett. Yes, that Billy Bennett—season twenty-two winner of *I Spy*. His dark hair and eyes and perfectly sculpted muscles won the hearts of ladies around the world. We met at the live show where he was crowned the winner. I was there with a friend; her husband was a producer on the show, and they needed to safely fill the live audience, so I volunteered.

I went home with him—stop judging me—and we were inseparable since that first day. We were also in the middle of a pandemic, so in hindsight, maybe we were both a little thirsty for human interaction. We married in Vegas two months later. It was fast, but we were living life because life is unpredictable. You only live once. Seize the day! And all that shit.

Plus, we were compatible. He was supportive of my career and understanding when I had to work long hours. And he loved tagging along to all the events with me. It was good enough for me.

She winces. "He'll be there with Kandi."

"Of course he will."

Kandi Kelly and Billy Bennett. They sound like they were meant to be. Kandi is also a reality star slash influencer slash beauty-brand mogul. I'm over my ex, but getting dumped for a gorgeous celebrity would fuck with anyone's self-esteem. Even worse, I'm the one who introduced them. He filed for divorce on Valentine's Day last year, claiming irreconcilable differences. We were together for less than two years, so it shouldn't have hurt as much as it did, but it was a friendly reminder that men are for fun, not forever.

"I need a plus-one," I say as I scroll through my contacts.

six

. . .

WYATT

LOST in my thoughts about seeing Blair again, I missed my floor and am stuck riding this elevator to the top, where my father sits with the other partners. Now I'll have to pretend it was intentional. There's no way he isn't here already. Maybe he'll be in a meeting, and I can fake that I forgot all about his schedule and then steal whatever homemade item his secretary, Pat, has made.

Well worth the unintentional detour.

"Wyatt! What brings you up here so early? You here to see your dad?" Pat comes around from her desk and heads straight to me with open arms. Even though she's nearly the same age as my dad, I think she's been playing the grandmother role her entire life. She's been supporting either my father or grandfather since she graduated college and is basically family at this point.

"Um, is he in his office?" I ask rather than confirm or deny my intentions.

"He sure is. You go on in there. He doesn't have any

appointments for another fifteen minutes." She pushes me toward his office, and while I know it's meant with love, it takes some restraint not to stand firm so I don't have to go in there.

"Wyatt? Did we have an appointment?" My father asks when he sees Pat usher me into his office.

"Oh, Jack, stop it. Your son does not need an appointment to say hi to his father."

Sweet and optimistic Pat. If only she knew how much he would prefer our conversations scheduled.

Actually, same.

"You mentioned a new client yesterday," I say. "Was just following up. How can I help?" I place my hands in my pockets to help stop me from fidgeting. This is so out of character for me, and I can see the skepticism splashed across his face when he squints his eyes.

I've been a disappointment to my father for as long as I can remember. Although, from the outside, you'd never know it. He loves to brag about his children, but if you listen closely, he's really just patting himself on the back for all we've accomplished.

"Did you hear Wyatt made law review? I knew when I set him up for the internship with my good friend, Judge Phillips, there was no way it wouldn't happen."

"He graduated top of his class! Good thing I had all those mentors and tutors on standby."

I was smart but not focused enough.

I was ambitious but not motivated enough.

I was social but not charming enough.

You see the pattern.

"You wanted to follow up." It's not a question. More of a statement of confirmed suspicion. "Sure. Pat should have already had your assistant put the meeting on the calendar, but the short version is TWA has accepted an offer to merge with The Manhattan Group. It'll be months before anything goes through, but TWA needs to clean some things up, tighten up spending, get rid of dead weight, you know, the usual housekeeping before everything is final."

I don't hear what he says next because all I can think about is that this assignment could mean another shot with Blair.

"I can take lead."

It's out of my mouth before I can take it back.

I don't know if I've ever seen my father speechless. Most days, I fight him on every account and spend all my effort avoiding working with him. I should have played this much cooler, but I had no fucking idea I would end up here first thing this morning. It's like I was thinking of Blair and the universe spit me out on the top floor and into the arms of a project that would allow me to see her again.

"I'll be lead, and Joe will handle the bulk of it. I wanted you to stay close for more experience with mergers and acquisitions," my father says as he stands, indicating the conversation is over.

I clench my fists, still in my pockets, and work to keep my face neutral.

"I've worked dozens of M&A cases, and you know that I'm the most experienced associate when it comes to entertainment clients." He knows I wanted to specialize in music and entertainment law, but that's not our family's legacy.

"Yes, I know. Unfortunately, I've let you waste too much of your time on frivolous work, and you're still not a partner at thirty. You'd think the name on the door would be compelling enough to take advantage of the cases I try to assign you."

My father is walking out the door, but now that I know the work will mean more time at the agency and with Blair, I pull out the only line I know will work—but also one I may come to regret.

"I've never asked you for any special treatment or favors. I'm asking for this. Make me lead, or at least second chair to you. I can handle this, and you know I'm the best suited for it, anyway."

"See you at the meeting," my father says as he vanishes around the corner.

I stand in his office, not knowing whether I've gotten through to him or, if I did, what it's going to cost me later.

seven

. . .

BLAIR

"HI, Lance. You here to see Blair?"

I hear Stella's voice project deliberately in warning outside my door as I slide my laptop into my oversized Prada Carolyn Shopper tote. As usual, she only gets a curt nod from the self-loving narcissist as he walks right by her.

Lance walks over to the couch in my office and makes himself right at home. "Leaving early again, I see. I'm glad I could catch you before you disappeared on me." He grabs a granola bar from the basket on the coffee table and leans back with a smirk, knowing I can't leave until he does.

"I'm headed out for the *Pink Slip* premiere. What can I help you with?" I sit back down at my desk, keeping my distance and the smile plastered on my face. I refuse to let him rattle me.

"I heard you went to see Sophia yesterday. My assistant said she secured passes for you."

"Yes, thanks again. It was a brief visit. Just building the relationship." I try to avoid sharing any details with him. He's smart. There's no way he doesn't realize I'm after her. As arrogant as Lance is, he respects the lanes. He knows that my signing Sophia is a win for everyone here so it won't be a competition.

"It'll be nice to see you sign someone. What's it been, almost a year since you've brought on a new client?"

Asshole. Getting current talent signed onto new projects is just as important as bringing in new talent.

"Is there something specific you need from me, Lance?"

A chuckle escapes his lips as he leans back and crosses his right leg over his left knee in his classic power pose. Lance is objectively handsome, but like many men in this business, he's compact. He claims to be five foot ten, which means closer to five foot eight or nine. He's slim but has more of a retired golfer's body, meaning he still does cardio but could stand to lift a few weights. He's very charming and has a black belt in Hollywood politics. I couldn't wait to work for him, and I loved it for a while until I made a mistake. Broke an unwritten rule. I tried to recover, but I learned quickly that I was never really on solid ground here, anyway. Nobody is. You're only as good as the success you are having right at this moment.

"Well, it's not public knowledge yet, but I trust you can keep a secret," Lance teases.

I don't respond.

"I'm sure you've heard the rumors from your little buddy Jess, but we have accepted an offer from The Manhattan Group. Assuming the board approves, and we get through the regulatory piece ok, we'll be a new company by the beginning of next year." Lance knows he just dropped a bomb, but what I can't figure out is why he's telling me this information.

"I hadn't heard. Jess is a professional. She would never share confidential information with me."

Actually, she might, but he doesn't need to know that.

I wonder if she knows this, though. She has shared clips of articles speculating that our financials in this current economic environment make us an ideal agency to purchase.

"With an official offer on the table, we're creating a task force. I was considering asking you to join. It would be good exposure for you with the new buyers. Unless you're too busy with other commitments. If it's not the right time..." He trails off for dramatic effect.

I despise him. He loves a good mind fuck. *I think you're good enough to be on the task force, but I don't want you to think that you're good enough to be on the task force.*

"Of course, I'm not too busy. I'd love to help any way I can." I offer nothing else and wait to see what he'll say next. He's quiet, too. It's a game of verbal chicken.

"Well, I guess you better get to the premiere. I can assign you to the task force for the exposure, but I'm not sure it will save your job if you can't sign talent. Good luck tonight."

He doesn't even wait for a response before he pops up from the couch and rushes out the door. He can bait me all he wants, but he knows I'm his best agent. He may not like my priorities and focus, but I brought in more money for this agency over the last five years than anyone else.

"Goodbye, Lance. Enjoy the rest of your afternoon..." Stella's voice trails off as she steps inside my office and closes the door. "Spill."

It's her job to listen in, so I know she heard the news. I recap for her what I know and ask her to get me details on The Manhattan Group. They are a sports management agency representing some of the biggest professional athletes. It makes sense for us to merge, and I'm optimistic there will be little fallout since both agencies focus on different things. There may be a few redundancies, but hopefully, the collateral damage will be minor. When the deal closes, we'll be the largest agency in media and sports.

eight

. . .

WYATT

"YOU LOOK GORGEOUS," I say when my sister walks out of her little bungalow in black silk pants and a black silk tank that seems to be missing a back. A hot pink scarf wrapped around her waist and matching heels complete the look. With her hair pulled up in a high ponytail, she looks like a modern Pink Lady from *Grease*. It's Bad Sandy meets Innocent Sandy.

"It's not too much?" She tilts her head from side to side. "Or too little?"

"It's perfect. You look like a fan of the show." I open the back door of the SUV that will take us to the premiere and motion for her to jump in.

"Is that a good thing or a bad thing?" she asks as she climbs in.

"Just take the compliment." I shake my head as I shut the door and then round the car to the other side. I'm all decked out in black, too. Apparently, it's the unofficial dress code for this premiere.

"Thanks for coming with me to this event," Sophia says to me when I get in, "but I didn't even ask you this time. Any particular reason you're so eager to be my plus-one?" She turns toward me, bringing her knee up on the seat like she's getting comfortable for girl talk.

We are most definitely not having girl talk.

I keep my eyes down on my phone, hoping she'll get the hint and change the topic.

"Come on, Wyatt. I have questions!"

To make it seem harmless, I decide to keep it simple. "There's not much to say. We were friends in high school, lost touch in college, and haven't talked since."

"Nuh-uh. There was shock, surprise, hunger, lust, anger, hurt, all the emotions swirling when you walked into my trailer yesterday." Sophia raises her elbow to lean on the back of the seat, doubling down on her interrogation.

I'm not sure what to tell her. It feels naïve to say I thought Blair was the love of my life. And until yesterday, I managed to block out those feelings, but then my heart betrayed me and started to convince me she could still be the love of my life. Now that we've seen each other, maybe she can be mine again?

I'm what the cool kids call delulu.

Seeing her again brought back so many memories. I had a crush on her when we first met. We slipped right into a comfort zone I've never had with anyone else, and it allowed us to grow as friends. But then her friend Holly came on strong and the three of us started spending time together. I was young, and she was a beautiful girl. When Blair seemed excited about Holly and me dating, I just assumed she was confirming our friend-zone status.

Holly was fun to date. She was a cheerleader and had the energy to play the part. But she liked it most when all eyes were on her. I'm pretty sure she cheated on me more than once, especially when we started to grow apart senior year. By that time, I didn't really care. I liked Holly, but I knew our relationship wouldn't last into college.

My parents spent the week with Sophia in LA for some auditions during Spring Break senior year, but I stayed back in Santa Barbara with my uncle to play in a qualifier event for an upcoming junior golf tournament. I ran into Blair on that first day of practice at the club. Turns out she wasn't going anywhere for spring break, either, so she could work extra shifts to save for college.

I'm not sure we even discussed it, but somehow, we ended up spending every bit of our free time together. She would run or work out with me in the mornings, and I would hang at the clubhouse until her shift was over. We would eat and watch TV together, and one night, I fell asleep at her house. That opened a door I didn't think I had the key to.

"Fine. You don't have to tell me, but I'm interested in her as an agent." Sophia pauses to see if I'll react. She knows I usually have an opinion about a lot of the things surrounding her career. When she got her big break, I was obsessed with the behind-the-scenes of it all. I foolishly thought our dad would be fine if I pursued entertainment law. As long as I was a lawyer, why would he care? I was so wrong. I tried to use every extra elective I could to take classes on intellectual property, distribution, trademarks, contracts—everything I could learn about the business behind Hollywood. I didn't get to practice that kind of law, but I definitely practice sharing my opinion on topics surrounding entertainment.

"She's one of the top agents in the industry," I tell Sophia. "You'd be in good hands." I may have looked her up a time or two to see what she was up to. I've seen the articles and awards she's won. It also means I've seen more about her than I wanted to know. She's not famous, but she was with a reality star who had a moment. There wasn't a magazine rack in town that spared me a view of her face when they got married.

"I'm not playing favorites. This is still a business decision. Even if you have history." Sophia straightens back up in her seat.

"I would never expect that. Neither would Blair. Let her court you and see if you think she's a fit."

"And you'll stay out of it?"

I give her a look that quickly communicates she should know better. I would never get involved like that.

"Ok, ok. I just needed to say it out loud so you know where I stand." She reaches over, grabs my hand, and gives it a squeeze.

"I would never try to influence something like that." I squeeze her hand back.

"I know. I'm not sure I will be as honorable. I'm invested in finding out if the love connection is still alive!" She laughs as we pull up to the theater.

"There's no love connection," I say too quickly and too harshly. Even I hear the defensive lie in my voice. "Look, I can't say a lot, but I'm working on a project, and TWA is the client. So, between you and work, there are plenty of conflicts of interest to keep Blair and me strictly professional."

She nods and pats me on the arm, her way of saying that she understands and won't push anymore...at least right now.

I join her outside the car and extend my elbow for her to wrap her arm around as we approach the red carpet.

"Besides," I say, "I don't even know if I'll see her again after tonight. We've been in this city for years without running into one another."

nine

. . .

BLAIR

I TRIED to convince Stella to join me tonight as my plus-one, but she ditched me for a yoga class. Instead, I beg Grant Hall, an exec at Wonderland Studios, to be my date. He's a good friend, and we have zero romantic interest in one another. We learned early on that we make great replacement dates for each other, though.

My divorce is old news, but with the rumor that the new happy couple will attend tonight, there's always a chance the press will ask if I've seen them or how I'm doing since the divorce. I hate that I care, but I don't want to go solo for fear of all that might imply: Sad. Alone. Pathetic.

Since this is a premiere featuring a female lead actor, director, and writer, I'd rather they ask questions about the female talent I represent, but that can be a sore spot, too.

Right around the time I was getting married, one of the top female stars we represent held a meeting with all of TWA's agency leads. She was getting typecast and wanted new ideas. I didn't know Lance was already in deep with

Everest Studios to lock the actress into a five-film deal with a new action franchise. She chose one of my ideas, and it killed the project at Everest. Lance was livid. He lost it. I'm pretty sure everyone heard him screaming that my "pussy-forward movement was a waste of everyone's time." That I was an idiot if I thought I could come in and really change this town's hundred-year legacy of filmmaking.

Trades caught wind of the gossip, and while they didn't have the exact details of what went down, there were murmurs I was on Lance's shit list.

I'm just finishing my makeup when I hear my phone buzz and see a text from Grant.

GRANT

Just arrived. Should I come to the door and pick you up like a proper date would?

ME

I'll be right out. No need to interrupt whatever call you're likely on.

GRANT

God, why can't you be my actual girlfriend? So understanding and low maintenance.

ME

Oh please, your work is your mistress. But I still love you.

GRANT

Ouch. Alright, back to work. See you shortly.

Twenty minutes later, we pull into the valet line at the Academy Museum of Motion Pictures and head over to the red carpet. As we walk toward the swarm of paparazzi and camera flashes, I spot Sophia and Wyatt. He's in all black. His pants are slim and hugging those thighs I seem to be obsessed with. He's in a button-down shirt with no tie and the top two buttons open. It looks like he hasn't shaved since yesterday, and it's just amping up the sex appeal.

He runs his hands through his hair as he searches the room and turns and sees me across the atrium. Our eyes lock for a minute before I watch him slide those steel-blue eyes up my dress and down again with a look of appreciation.

It reminds me of when we first met. When we looked at each other, it was like we were hypnotized. It took too long for us to stop staring at one another. He was so beautiful. Every time he came to the clubhouse after a round of golf, he would make it a point to sit in my section, and we'd talk until he had to leave or my shift was up.

But then I saw Holly sitting at his table, and her hands were all over him. I saw how he looked at her and laughed with her, and I immediately backed off. I was convinced I'd misread my connection with Wyatt and shifted my desire for him into the biggest champion for the two of them to date.

I break eye contact and look around the red carpet to see if my ex is here. Thankfully, there's no sign of him.

Grant places his hand on my lower back and guides me to the edge of the carpet, next to Sophia and Wyatt. Wyatt watches Grant's hand and flicks his eyes to me as his jaw tenses.

"Blair, so nice to see you again," Wyatt says.

Sophia turns with a smile on her face and immediately pulls me into a hug.

"Thank you so much for the passes. I'm obsessed with this show!" She says.

"Of course! Sophia, I wanted to introduce you to Grant Hall. He's head of creative at Wonderland Studios. Grant, this is Sophia Ford."

Grant takes Sophia's hand, and she gets his full attention, which is surprising since he's usually distracted by all the noise.

"Even more beautiful in person. Sophia, I'm honored to meet you."

Sophia immediately blushes, and I catch Wyatt rolling his eyes as he turns away.

"And this is Sophia's brother, Wyatt."

Grant reaches out to shake Wyatt's hand.

"Nice to meet Blair's other half," Wyatt spits out, almost angry.

I think my mouth drops open, but thankfully, Grant steps in to answer.

"Oh, we're not together. Blair and I have been good friends since she started at TWA." He smiles at Wyatt. "I don't think it's a good idea to mix business and pleasure, but if I did, she'd definitely be one to catch." Grant gives me a wink, and I snap my mouth shut for fear I'll say something I regret.

Wyatt gives me another look to see if I'll confirm that fact, and I offer him a small smile, along with a slight look of rage. He nods and places his hand on Sophia's back to escort her down the carpet.

"Someone's jealous," Grant whispers in my ear.

"He's not jealous. He's nosy. I'm trying to sign Sophia,

and he's playing the protective-older-brother game." Hopefully, Grant doesn't notice how I keep glancing at Wyatt. It's a dead giveaway that I'm excited at the idea that Wyatt could be jealous.

"Ok. Whatever you say." Thankfully, Grant drops the topic. "Sophia seems nice. I've not had the chance to work with her yet." I watch his gaze follow her down the carpet.

I would think more of it, but he rarely dates—even less now that he has full custody of his six-year-old daughter.

Grant and I make our way down the red carpet, and just when I think I'm in the clear, a journalist stops me as we're stepping off the line. I tell Grant to go on in and I'll catch up with him. Thankfully, it's a simple question about the ladies in *Pink Slip*. It's a quick exchange, but the distraction means I don't realize Billy and Kandi have arrived and are right behind me until it's too late.

"Baby girl! How are you? So good to see you." He kisses me on both cheeks in the most pretentious way as I awkwardly try to lean away from him. "You know Kandi, right?"

I twist my lips into what I hope is a smile and realize that I'm only nodding my head. I look around and notice all the flashes and cameras facing our way and start to panic. The last thing I want is to be photographed with them. Why did I send Grant away?

Kandi places her arms around his neck and leans in to kiss him—I'm guessing to claim him because she thinks my silence is jealousy. I should say something, but my mind is blank. When I'm about to turn and run from the scene, I feel a hand on my elbow, and it's Wyatt, smiling at the photographers.

"Excuse me for interrupting. I need to steal this beauty away for a minute." He puts his arm around my waist and places a kiss on my temple as he guides me through the crowd. We walk into the nearest bathroom, and once we're inside, he turns to lock the door, and his arm traps me against it.

He bends down to look into my eyes, and his hand comes under my chin, lifting my face so I'm looking at him.

"You ok?"

"Yeah. Thank you." I push off the door because having him that close to my body makes everything inside me feel like fireworks. I tell myself it's the adrenaline from seeing Billy and Kandi, but teenage Blair is giddy as fuck right now.

"I don't know why I froze out there. I knew they would be here." I walk over to the sink and check my makeup and hair in the mirror. My eyes dart to look at him in the reflection. He's leaning against the door with his hands casually in his pockets. I can't tell what he thinks, so I keep talking.

"It's just embarrassing when your failures get photographed and splashed all over the gossip magazines. I hate it and try to avoid it at all costs."

He just smiles and then pushes off the door. His steps feel like slow motion until he's standing beside me. He reaches out to tuck a loose lock of hair behind my ear.

"I wouldn't consider the split with Billy a failure, but I understand what you're saying."

His hand is still resting on my shoulder, and I can't tear my gaze from his right now. When his eyes dip to peek at my lips, it's easy to forget all about how much he hurt me and instead I imagine what his lips would feel like on mine.

A knock at the door pulls us out of our trance.

"We should get back out there." I walk to the door. "I'm sure Sophia and Grant are wondering where we are."

"She sent a text a few minutes ago. She's headed into the theater with your friend Grant." His eyebrows raise as he emphasizes "your friend."

"Grant is harmless."

"He looks comfortable with you."

"He is," I say. I won't apologize for having good relationships with male colleagues. "We're just friends."

I can feel Wyatt's body against my back as he reaches around to open the door for me.

"Good."

My heart races again, and I need to get these butterflies under control. We've both obviously moved on. What happened was so long ago, and even though we were friends first, what we had was just a fling. Besides, I'm trying to land his sister as a client. I need to keep everything professional.

When we exit the bathroom, he reaches down and laces his fingers through mine. It's hilarious how quickly I fold on my stance to stay professional. I shake it off and assume it's all for the crowd of reporters and photographers still around, just a friendly gesture. He's just helping me out, taking one for the team.

Whatever you need to tell yourself, Blair.

We make our way into the theater, and I shiver as he places his hand on my lower back to guide us to our seats. Since we are the last ones to show up in our section, I'm now sitting next to him instead of Grant. Sophia and Grant are a few seats down and she leans forward and looks over me to ask Wyatt what took so long. Her gaze darts back and forth at us both.

"Lines for the bathroom were long," Wyatt says.

I smile at her awkwardly, hoping it looks like I'm confirming his lie.

The lights go down, and the show begins, but all I can focus on is Wyatt's thigh pressed against my knee. He moves his elbow to the edge of the armrest, leaving space for my arm, but my attention is fixed on how big his hands look resting on his leg. I immediately hate how my body betrays the pep talk about professionalism I just gave myself.

Swallowing the desire, I focus on trying to make it through the next fifty minutes.

ten

. . .

WYATT

I GRAB a drink from the bar and scan the room to find Blair. She's talking to the talent, and as I watch her, she throws her head back in laughter. God, that makes my dick twitch. She's so gorgeous. All I wanted to do in that theater was slide my hands up her thighs and see if she was as excited to sit next to me as I was to be sitting next to her.

She looks around the room, and our eyes lock when she spots me. She offers a small, professional smile, and I take it greedily, giving her one in return.

I've missed her.

There's a lightness in my chest I haven't felt in years.

Sophia comes up and bumps my elbow. It catches me off guard, and I almost spill my drink.

"What's got you distracted?" It's a rhetorical question because I see her look directly at Blair. The same place I'm looking. "Grant speaks highly of her; says she's got a great reputation."

"That doesn't surprise me one bit," I say.

"I'm excited to spend more time with her."

Sophia is talented and works hard at her craft. She's hot right now, but she earned every bit of it. Blair wasn't wrong when she mentioned how quickly attention shifts in this town, so I know it's important that she sign with someone who understands her drive and dreams.

I also agree Blair would be a good fit for her, and I know I'm biased, but from what I've read, she is respected, and some of the heavy hitters in this industry have turned to her for opinions, deals, and more. She was always ambitious. I knew she'd be successful.

I know my opinion is important to Sophia, and I also know she won't hesitate to override it if she disagrees with me. But right now, my honest thoughts are that I'd like to be more than a professional acquaintance to Blair, and I worry that if Sophia signs with her, I'll have struck out before even getting a chance to take a swing.

"I can look through any contracts, of course, but you both have the same passion for storytelling," I say. "Do the due diligence, but if it feels good. Go for it."

"Thanks, Wyatt. I appreciate that." She hugs me and then pulls back to straighten my shirt collar.

I bring the glass of whiskey to my lips and gaze at Blair. Grant walks up behind her, places his hand on her hip, and gives her a light peck on the cheek.

"You have a death grip on that glass, big brother."

Sophia knowingly pats me on the arm and lets me know she'll catch up with me soon. I place my drink on a nearby table so I have an excuse to grab another at the bar next to Blair. While I wait for the bartender, I turn to make sure she's still in conversation nearby, but then I see she's walking toward me. She's stopped along the way by people who reach out to hug her and say hello. Clearly, she's loved by many in this town.

Her confidence is sexy as hell, and I have a hard time keeping my eyes on hers. Tonight, her lips are pink, and she has on more makeup, but you can still see a small sprinkle of freckles across her nose and cheeks. She's wearing her hair down, and I remember how my hands felt combing through those layers.

I need to save these thoughts for home.

"How did you like the show?" she asks as she raises her empty glass of champagne to the bartender, signaling for another. She doesn't focus on me; instead, her gaze roams the room.

"Better than I thought I would." It's not really my genre, but it was good writing.

"That's high praise coming from someone who was obsessed with *Suits* when we were in high school." She's teasing me.

"Hey, it's making a comeback. It's very validating," I joke.

"I'll admit, I'm impressed, Blair. You've really done well for yourself. I'm happy for you." Her head bobs gently, acknowledging the compliment, but then I watch her pull her shoulders back with confidence.

"Thanks. Seems you've done well, too."

According to my father, it's an utter disappointment that I'm not yet a partner. He has worked hard to architect every part of my professional life, so I'm not sure why he hasn't pushed to make that happen. I don't care, and he wants me to care, so we're at a stalemate.

"Everything my father ever wanted." It comes out harsher than I mean for it to. I can tell by the way she raises her eyebrows and locks her eyes with mine that she wants to question that comment but won't.

We stand next to each other, looking out at the party, neither of us talking. A scream of laughter pulls our heads in the same direction, and I see her ex taking a shot off of his new wife's belly while she's stretched out on the bar.

"How'd that happen?" I ask. "He doesn't seem like your type."

"Temporary insanity." She's joking, but I want to know more, so I don't look away. "Pandemic, isolation. I was lonely, and the world was ending."

It's not an answer, but it doesn't sound like she's upset that it's over.

My brain takes me down a cruel spiral of wondering how many Billys there were after me. She has an Instagram account, but it only has two pictures on it: her parents visiting her freshman year in college and a group of friends I don't know from that same year.

One night during my freshman year at UCLA, I went on an internet deep dive, looking for anything I could find about Blair. When I couldn't find anything on her account, I searched her name and found some posts where she was tagged in some girl named Jess's pictures. Most of the pics were group shots with her girlfriends, except one.

There was some guy with his hand wrapped around her waist. She was turned toward him with her head tilted back, looking up at him with a huge smile on her face. It haunts me to this day. I must have stared at that photo for days, studying their faces. I obsessed over where his hands were on her waist. Were his fingers digging into her side too deeply? Were his hips twisted toward her because they were dating? Was she laughing at something he said? Was she sleeping with him?

I wanted to go see her immediately, but she was on the East Coast. I knew I couldn't drive or fly without my parents knowing. They wanted to make sure I had no distractions while in college, so they funded my entire life so I didn't have to work. I know I was lucky, but it also meant I had no control over anything because every move I made was monitored.

I lean down and whisper in her ear, "He'll soon learn that losing you was the biggest mistake of his life."

I see her shiver, and I hope it's because she enjoys feeling me close to her. I wonder if she can sense how much I miss her. I see Grant walking our way, and I straighten back up and put some space between us.

"Hey, I need to head out," Grant says. "Hazel lost a tooth, and I want to see her before she falls asleep."

"I can give you a ride home," I say.

They look at me like I've interrupted something private between them. I realize too late that I've offered before I even know if she needs a ride.

"I mean, if you need a ride, I can... There's room in our car."

"I can call a car service," Blair says.

"It sounds like I don't have to feel guilty for taking off,

then?" Grant asks her. She tells him she's fine and hugs him goodbye.

"I have a driver," I tell her. "It's no problem at all.".

I want to take her home. I just want a little more time with her. I tell her it will also give her more time with Sophia since we rode together. She hesitates, as though struggling with the implication that she might be taking advantage of the situation until Sophia walks up and tells her she was excited to hear from Grant that we're giving her a ride home.

eleven

. . .

BLAIR

THE SILENCE in this car is killing me. We've said nothing to each other since we dropped Sophia off and I gave him my address ten minutes ago.

"So, do you like—"

"Do you remember—"

We both start talking at the same time and then laugh.

"Do I remember...what, exactly?" I ask him cautiously. This feels like stepping into our sticky past.

"It's actually who. That big guy who used to help load all the golf bags onto the carts. Henry, I think his name was?"

"Yes! I haven't thought about him in years! He was so nice, but also the weirdest person I've ever met." I turn to face him, and he's already adjusted in his seat to face me.

"He's a motivational speaker now."

"NO! You're lying."

"Swear it. My buddy Jake is into all that self-improvement stuff. I saw him onstage." He tells me about his yearly trip with his buddies and how, two years ago, Jake made them all go to an "Attract Your Ideal Mate" session. Wyatt saw the poster board sign for the session in the room next to his, and it was Harry.

He pulls up a photo from his phone and shows me, and I'm taken right back to senior year. God, we had so much fun. We were so close. I didn't think I would love anyone else but him. It's fascinating how completely blind you are as a young adult. You really believe you know everything, and you can't realize how much you don't understand yet. How much life you absolutely haven't experienced.

That deep thought has me shifting to face forward in my seat again.

"What made you think of that?" I ask him. It's a pretty random reference, considering all of the memories from our past that he could have chosen from—or of high school in general.

"I think about that time more than I should." He stares straight ahead, but I see him lick his lips and swallow like he's nervous.

"We don't need to walk down memory lane, Wyatt. We were best friends. I don't regret being with you, but it's all in the past. We've moved on. We're different people now." I wave him off because I thought I'd moved on, but in this car with him, after feeling his hands briefly touch my body a few innocent times tonight, every memory is bombarding me.

"What if I haven't?"

"Haven't what?" I look at him, confused.

"Moved on."

I laugh at him because it's absurd to think the guy who

literally slept with me and then got right back together with his girlfriend hasn't moved on.

"Yeah, I can tell. All the letters, texts, and phone calls have been too much." I'm joking with him because I can't even get into this. I don't want him to think I'm not over it—or that it affected me as much as it did. And I'm definitely not talking about this with him.

"I couldn't," Wyatt says.

"Couldn't what?" I ask, truly confused about what that is supposed to mean. Couldn't call me? Couldn't make contact at all? I go from angry to hurt to confused in a matter of seconds.

"Nothing. You're right. It's in the past."

I look over and watch his shoulders stiffen. I think the thing that bothers me most is how I was so wrong about him. About us. I want to know what happened. He treated me with such care and patience, and I believed we both wanted to be together. What changed? Why wasn't I enough?

"I'm sorry, Blair."

I wait for him to say something more, but he doesn't. Then his comfort shifts to detachment. I just stare and push my lips together in a tight smile. I don't want him to know how much he hurt me. Thankfully, perfect timing means we've arrived at my house.

"Thank you so much for the ride home." I open the door to get away from this completely awkward conversation, but he jumps out and rushes to help me out of the car. I hesitate because, while I don't need his help, I seem to want to torture myself.

When I go to stand, my heel catches in my dress, and I

fall right into him. One hand lands on his bicep, and the other slams into his chest. I feel his muscles flex as he grabs me, and my stomach drops. I can feel the outline of his pecks under his shirt, and it takes all my willpower not to run my hand down his chest to his abdomen.

"Careful. You ok?" His face is so close to mine that I can feel his breath on my lips. I look up, but he's staring at my lips, and the memories rush back and make it seem as if no time has passed. I lean in, and so does he.

I feel his hands adjust around my waist, and that's all it takes for me to snap out of it. My hands pull away like I've been burned, and I step back, making sure my dress is clear of my shoes.

"Thanks for the ride, Wyatt. Have a good night."

I run up the steps to my front door as fast as possible to get away from whatever that was. After rushing through the front door, I close it and immediately look out the peephole.

He's standing with his hands in his pockets, staring at my house. After a minute, he turns to get back into his car, and I swear I see a smile take over his lips. I turn around and slide down my front door until I'm sitting on the floor.

Thanks for the ride? Smooth, Blair. Jesus.

twelve

. . .

BLAIR

"TO WOMEN RULING THE WORLD!" Jess yells as she raises her glass. It's been a week since the almost lip slip with Wyatt, and I needed a distraction so I'd stop thinking about it. Drinks with the ladies seemed like a perfect idea.

We ran into Brandon at the bar, so we invited him to join our little group. It seems I was the last one to meet him. He lives in the same building as Jess and Stella, so no introductions were needed.

"No offense, Brandon!" Stella quickly adds in. She's always so good about making sure everyone feels loved and included.

"None taken. I love women, and even more when they are ruling my world." He winks back at Stella, and she blushes. He's good.

"Ok, so now what?" Jess asks me, pulling the olives out of her martini glass. I don't know why she orders them when she'll never touch one.

"Well, off the record," I say pointedly to my journalist friend, "I just read a script from Edie Lang. It's a passion project for her that TWA won't look at or doesn't want to shop—I'm not sure what the full story is yet."

I caught up with Edie while getting coffee yesterday morning. She keeps pushing more female-forward stories to her agent, Brian, but he keeps pushing back on her for more traditional box-office stories. Edie made her name in the business writing your favorite sci-fi movies.

"So, what does that mean?" Brandon asks.

Everyone looks knowingly at each other and then at me to explain.

"That he'd rather have her keep writing sci-fi. There's a level of comfort and history of success." I explain that, technically, Edie's agent should shop all her scripts around to producers or studios, but in this business, agents are just as likely to sweep work aside to focus on the bigger ideas. I give Brandon the 101 on agency life and explain that one of my colleagues, Brian, represents Edie. Since we work for the same agency, I could offer ideas or possibly even mention in passing to a producer that she's looking to sell a project. But "agency code" says Brian would need to approve.

Ideally, Brian would approve and let me help sell the shit out of her ideas to every studio in Hollywood. He is the luckiest agent I've ever met. He has a few well-placed contacts that have allowed him to coast and succeed brilliantly. It's looking more and more like it could have been a fluke with Edie since he continues to push her to write more sci-fi and hasn't been able to sell any of her other original ideas.

"So, could you ask Brian if you could help with Edie?" Stella asks. She knows that's exactly what I want to do, but it's a delicate dance.

And now, with the possibility of a merger, virtual knives will be out. People panic when career stability is a threat. Once Lance announces the intention of The Manhattan Group, the first question will be about layoffs.

"That would be the ideal solution." I finish my drink and wave the server over for the check. "Which is why I must leave now. I have a date with my bed, a dozen scripts, and leftover pizza."

Jess hugs me and heads out to finish up some work she's on deadline for as well, but Stella and Brandon decide to hang back for one more drink.

"You two be safe," I say. "I'll see you in the morning."

"I'll make sure she gets home safe," Brandon says. I laugh because his reply is filled with innuendo that makes Stella shift awkwardly in her seat. I wave goodbye, and as I'm heading to my car, my phone buzzes with a text from an unknown number.

UNKNOWN

Can you meet me at Firefly at 8pm?

ME

Who is this?

UNKNOWN

Wyatt. I got your number from Sophia.

Why is he asking me to meet him at a restaurant—and a nice one at that? Is he asking me to dinner?

UNKNOWN

I'm not asking you on a date.

UNKNOWN

Official business.

UNKNOWN

Working dinner.

Does he mean Sophia? She already seemed suspicious when I didn't immediately tell her I knew her brother.

ME

Is that fair?

UNKNOWN

You're worried about fair in this town?

Good point. If it were anyone else, I would gladly meet up for some info that could help me gain an advantage.

ME

Ok. See you soon.

thirteen

. . .

BLAIR

I **PULL** up to the restaurant an hour later and check my makeup in the rearview mirror. I had a few meetings this morning, so at least I look nice since there was no time to go home and change. The hostess leads me through the restaurant until we are in the outdoor courtyard.

I see Wyatt, but he's not alone. A gorgeous blonde is sitting at his table with her hand resting on his forearm. She looks comfortable as she leans in, leading the conversation, and he's just as relaxed with a smile on his face.

I stop the hostess and tell her I need to run to the restroom. Yes, I'm totally hiding from him until I can get the confidence to interrupt his lovefest, but I ask her to let Wyatt know I'm here and will join him shortly. I step inside the bathroom and try to shake this weird, anxious feeling that feels a lot like jealousy.

Just then, the gorgeous blonde from his table walks through the door. She smiles at me on her way to a bathroom stall. She's glamorous, with more of an edge. More crisp and designed than most women. She's in a fitted, suit-style gray dress with buttons down the front and a thin belt around her even thinner waist. Slight and tall, she looks like a Victoria's Secret model.

Of course, he likes her. What's not to like? She looks like the Barbie to his Ken.

I wash my hands quickly and head out to meet up with Wyatt. I'm having second thoughts about coming here and looking like the sloppy seconds next on his list. He notices me approaching and quickly stands to welcome me with a hug, but I dodge him and rush to sit down.

"Thanks for meeting me for dinner. I know it was last minute. Can I get you a glass of wine or something else to drink?" He sits and motions for our server.

"Chardonnay," I snap.

While he orders, I see the blonde leaving the restroom, and I look back at him to see if he notices. If he does, he doesn't let on.

"So, who was the gorgeous woman you were meeting with before me?" I can't help it. My curiosity is killing me.

"Oh, um, she's a colleague from New York." He looks uncomfortable. Was he on a date?

"I thought you said you had a client meeting?"

"I don't recall mentioning a meeting?" He looks at me with raised eyebrows. "Why are you so curious?"

"I'm not. Let's talk Sophia." I try to get us back on track, hoping that I didn't sound like a jealous girlfriend asking him where he's been all night.

"Sure. No problem." He looks at me with a knowing grin,

and I hope to hell the flush on my cheeks isn't visible in the darkened dining area.

Apparently, he already ordered food for us, as the server drops off a small, cast-iron skillet of meatballs drowning in the most delicious red sauce I've ever smelled. There are also Manzella olives, a light but crispy French bread, and a farmers' market salad to share. I wonder if Jess would eat these olives. They have to be the best thing I've tasted all year.

"I tried to order a few things I thought you might like," he tells me. "But please, order anything else."

I glance at the menu and put it back down. He's chosen exactly the same things I would have picked for myself.

"This looks great for now. Thank you."

"What can I tell you about Sophia? You already know her history. She wants to produce and direct, and she'll push you to find those projects." Wyatt takes a drink of his wine, and I can't help but watch his throat as he swallows.

No more wine for me.

"She's young, and she's still considered new. But if that's what she wants, I'm committed to figuring out how to make that happen for her."

Sophia made the jump from teen sensation to Oscar winner. It seems to some like she's an "overnight success." Many actors have years of experience in major films and several awards on their shelves before stretching their talent into other areas of this business. But if anyone can cross the unwritten barriers in this industry, she can.

"We can talk more about Sophia, but there's something else I need to tell you." He straightens in his chair, shifting to a more professional demeanor.

This is where he probably tells me not to get my hopes up because she's already been talking to other agents. Maybe he's friendly with other agents and set her up with someone amazing. I bet it's Alan over at DCA. He's good, but I still think I'm a better match for her.

"Where'd you go?" Wyatt asks.

"Sorry, go ahead. I'm listening." I prepare for the letdown.

"So, my firm has just taken TWA on as a new client." He looks at me like I might know this information, or maybe he wants me to share information.

"Congratulations?"

The question in my voice makes him hesitate. "It's just. Well, it's possible we could see more of each other, and I wanted to make sure we're on the same page."

Same page? What does that mean? I stay silent and wait for him to elaborate.

"It's just...we probably shouldn't cross any boundaries," he says.

Oh, hell no.

I cross my arms and lean back in my chair. He shifts in his chair as the realization sets in that maybe he's made some assumptions about our boundaries.

"I'm not saying we would. Jesus. This is coming out all wrong."

"I think we're on the same page, Wyatt." I down the rest of my wine. "I should get going. I look forward to seeing you around the office." I stand.

"Wait, you're leaving? Why? We've not even finished dinner. There's still dessert."

There's no way I can sit through another half-hour with him so he can tell me more about these boundaries he's eager to keep. This was a mistake to meet him tonight. I know better. I'm furious, but only at myself. He's actually being the only professional at this table, and apparently, I've gotten too comfortable with him—so comfortable he's having a fucking boundaries conversation with me. I scream that last part in my head.

"It's actually probably better for me to skip those calories." I force a laugh.

"Blair, wait. At least let me pay the check and walk you out."

I turn away from him and let out a small sigh. "I'm going to the ladies' room, and I'll meet you up front."

When I walk to the lobby, I see Wyatt talking to the woman who was at his table earlier. I didn't realize she was still here. She's hanging on his every word as he charms her with his stupid velvet voice and stupid good looks. I wonder if she's aware of his "professional boundaries." Or maybe she is why he mentioned them to me.

I've got to get out of here. While he's got his back to me, I sneak out the front door and leave without saying goodbye. I tell myself I'm setting my own boundaries. The less time I spend with Wyatt, the easier it will be to keep him off my mind, out of my heart, and firmly in my past.

Ten minutes later, I hear my phone ding , and my car reads the text aloud.

"Message from Wyatt. Did you leave?"

I press the speaker button on my steering wheel to reply.

"Yes. Driving. Can't text."

I wait a few minutes, and when he doesn't respond, my shoulders relax, and I sigh. I tell myself I'm relieved, but I wonder if it just means that he's the one relieved, so he could leave with his Barbie.

I finally get into my bed, cozy in my favorite offensive "what the actual fuck" T-shirt. It's exactly the vibe I'm feeling tonight. I grab my glass of wine and stack of scripts, and just as I begin to read, I hear my phone buzz on my nightstand.

WYATT

It was nice to see you tonight. Maybe we can grab coffee once I'm working at your office?

Are you fucking kidding me?

I leave him on read.

I lie back in my bed, full of disdain, jealousy, and confusion. I need to get these emotions in check. I'm not interested. I know better. And even if I were, he's off limits. He made that loud and clear.

fourteen

. . .

WYATT

"**DON'T** bachelor parties normally start much later?" I ask Jake.

We've just made it to a seven a.m. tee time, and while I love a good foursome, I'd like it much more if it were ten a.m. I feel sorry for Jake. Our Manmorial weekend is now doubling as his bachelor party. "Two birds, one stone," according to his fiancé, Lauren.

"Sorry, man." Jake offers me an apologetic smile. "Best I could do if we want to fit everything in."

I'm trying my best to be happy for Jake, but Lauren can be a challenge. He proposed last year, but she's always had an excuse for why they can't set a wedding date just yet. Now, suddenly, she's found a date and a location, and not only is it a month away, it's on the fucking Fourth of July. She's excited to have fireworks as the co-star of the event. Now she's convinced Jake that our annual guy's trip to San Diego could double as his bachelor party so he won't have to leave town twice before the wedding.

"So, you gonna tell me what's going on with you?" Jake steps out of the cart and heads toward his clubs in the back. He doesn't even give me a chance to dodge his question. I put the brake on and meet him at the back as he grabs his driver out of his bag.

"I saw Blair."

I'm not sure why I keep my eyes focused on the tee box. Maybe so he can't see my excitement, the torture of it all, or that I'm absolutely gone for her? He's quiet for a minute, so I know he understands.

I can't get Blair out of my head—mostly the way I stupidly doubled down on keeping everything professional. At first, I thought I saw a look of hurt, and I hoped it was because maybe she wanted something more. Then I quickly realized that I had insulted her and it's quite possible she hates me. Talk about a gut punch.

Blair has haunted my thoughts for years. I dated in college, but Jake used to get so frustrated every time I ended it with a girl after a few dates. He would tell me I was romanticizing the past. He begged me to give any girl a real chance and stop comparing her to Blair. He said I was probably just a blip on her romantic resume.

Jake takes his place in the tee box and bends over to place the ball on the little peg sticking out of the ground.

"So, what's the plan, then?" he asks as he takes a few practice swings to get a feel for his shot.

"Plan? There's no plan. She's trying to sign my sister. I ran into her when I had lunch with Sophia the other day." I conveniently leave out dinner the other night.

"So, that's it? You see the woman you've been obsessed with since we met in college, and now what? You'll just go back to normal and not see her again?" He chuckles. Like a jolly old fellow.

"Not exactly," I say.

Jake just nods and strikes the ball, sending it sailing toward the first hole.

"So, I'll ask again, what's the plan?"

"I asked to be assigned to work on The Manhattan Group and TWA merger," I tell him. He may not realize our firm is helping, but he knows the deal I'm referring to. He also knows Blair works for TWA. He gives me a curious grunt.

"But I told her there was nothing to worry about and that we'd keep things totally professional."

He raises an eyebrow at me. "Because there was something to worry about?"

"Well, no. But I wanted her to know I'm a professional. I wouldn't let lingering feelings or our past impede our relationship."

"You have a relationship?" He's got both hands on the end of the club propped in front of him. His lawyer is showing.

"No. We don't..." I say. "*Working* relationship. I just thought it would set her mind at ease in case we have to work together. I don't have any expectations."

"Except complete professionalism."

"Fuck. I'm such an asshole." I wipe my hand down my face and then move past him to place my ball on the tee.

That's why she left our dinner without saying goodbye. I

completely insinuated there might be feelings—likely from her—and it looked like I was shutting it down. I'm such an idiot. I was so excited to see her again and doing my best to rein in my own feelings—apparently in the worst possible way.

After a day of golf and a few private poker games, we're headed to a Cage Warriors MMA matchup. It's the main reason we're celebrating Jake's bachelor party here this weekend. He's a huge fan and, in another life, would have loved to pursue it as a career.

My phone buzzes as we take our seats, and I'm about to shut it off when I see my sister's name flash across the screen.

SOPHIA

Sorry to interrupt man weekend, but can you send me Blair's address?

ME

Why?

SOPHIA

I want to send her a thank you for the tickets.

I forward over the contact info and then scroll back through the few messages between me and Blair. If I sent her a text asking about her weekend, I wonder if she would leave me delivered or on read—or tell me to fuck off.

"What's got you smiling? Or who?" Jakes asks.

"Nothing. Just Sophia."

"Listen, man, I know there's unfinished history with Blair, and the idea of opening up again probably scares the hell out of you. Love means being vulnerable, but I'm telling you it's worth it. I know things are complicated, but if there's a chance to reignite that spark, why not take it? Don't live with a second round of regret. Love is worth it, my friend, every single time."

He's only heard me talk about her a few times, yet he knows how much she meant to me. He also knows how much I regret not fighting for her, for us. I shared with him what I went through with my father. My passion for golf, my interest in something other than following in his footsteps. How he blamed Blair, and I didn't defend her.

I shut down after the blowout with my father and focused on school. I know I pulled away from her, but it was too painful to be around her and listen to her tell me how all my dreams could come true, because they wouldn't.

When it happened, everything felt so impossible. But then, a year later—and what felt like a lifetime of emotion later—everything seemed like no big deal. Insignificant. I couldn't believe what a coward I had been. Jake wanted me to call her and tell her what had happened. But I never did. I didn't even know what I would say to her. There's no way she would have understood, and by the time my head was in the right place, too much time had passed.

"I don't think this is exactly a second chance, but I hear you. I just think right now, the best thing I can do for both of us is stay professional and keep us focused on work."

"Right. Work." He raises his eyebrow with a look that says bullshit.

Thankfully, he drops it, and we get our drinks just in time to see the first punch. I'd been looking forward to the fight for a few weeks, but now my attention was miles away. About 120 miles, to be exact.

fifteen

. . .

BLAIR

THE BREEZE BLOWS through my hair as I walk to the front doors of TWA's offices. June gloom is officially in full effect. At least it's warm. Some people complain about not getting four seasons, but I find immense joy in perfect temperatures year-round.

As I'm peeking at my reflection in the window and running my fingers through my hair one last time, I see Wyatt walk up behind me.

I haven't seen him since his declaration of professionalism over a professional dinner he probably put on his very professional corporate card.

"Hey, let me get that for you," Wyatt says.

I can feel the warmth from his breath on my cheek as we reach for the door at the same time. There's a flutter in my chest at just the idea of his arms around me, and I try to shake it off. That excitement quickly turns to frustration since all I can hear is the replay of his adamant protest about professionalism.

I'll show him professional.

"Thanks."

My pace picks up as I cross the lobby. It's as if the faster I walk, the faster I can outrun any feelings for him. It's not working because I can hear him right behind me and my memory didn't get the memo that we're not reminiscing about this guy.

If I thought the front door was painful, then the elevator ride is excruciating. We're the only ones in the small enclosure, and as much as I try to keep my eyes on the display showing the passing floors, I can't help but steal a glance or two at his blurred reflection in the metal doors. He's staring at me, and I look away as if my eyes just committed a felony.

The way he looks is a felony.

Just as he's turning toward me, the doors open and reveal Lance waiting for the elevator. I introduce him to Wyatt, and awareness flits across his eyes as guilt flashes on his face. At least, I think it's guilt because that's not an emotion I see much from Lance. As I move to excuse myself, I hear Lance mention that I'll be working with Wyatt.

"I'm sorry, what?" I say, confused.

"We talked about this," Lance says. "Remember? Visibility."

What we talked about was a thinly veiled threat that I may or may not make it through this merger. And how he might do me a favor by including me in the meetings, but I haven't received any invites. I'm guessing he forgot he was supposed to meet with Wyatt, so now I'm conveniently invited to participate.

"Right. Happy to help," I say with my best fake smile.

"Great. My assistant can show you where meetings are today and pass along any info you need. It was great to meet you, Wyatt. Blair is an incredible resource and here to make sure you have everything you need. I'll catch up with you both later. I've got to run."

He gives Wyatt a handshake and ignores me as he jumps onto the elevator. As I head to his office to figure out what the plan for the day is, I pull out my phone to text Stella an update.

"Hey, wait up." I hear Wyatt quicken his steps behind me. "What was that about?"

I don't have time to answer before we arrive at Katie's desk and she immediately notices the man to my left.

"Hi, Blair! If you're here to see Lance, you just missed him. I don't think he had time blocked for you today."

She's looking at her computer to see if she's missed something. Then she gazes up at Wyatt while tucking her hair behind her ear and dragging her hand down to her chest. She's totally flirting with him. "Um, who is your guest?"

Before I can explain anything, he reaches out to shake Katie's hand.

"Hi, I'm Wyatt from Bradford and Associates. I'm here for Project Skyscraper."

I watch as this entire exchange happens.

Katie blushes when his big, powerful hands engulf hers. They wrap around her wrist, and I wonder if they would still swallow mine in the same way. Her chin drops, and she blushes—her cheeks actually turn a shade of crimson—and he's only just said hello to her. He leans on the counter that separates us from her workstation.

"Project Skyscraper?" I ask. Are we actually using code names?

He looks over, and before he can respond, Katie jumps in, all knowing and gathering folders and documents to pass over to him. "Blair, I don't see you on the invite. Did you need something else?"

"Lance just asked me to join the meeting. We saw him at the elevator."

Katie gets a knowing look in her eye. I'll give it to her. She knows her boss and understands the dynamics of how to manage him.

"Of course. Right this way. I'll bring you both down to the room reserved for the project."

Once we're in the conference room, Katie tells Wyatt to let her know if we need anything and places her hand on his biceps. A spark of something that feels like irritation grips me, but I can't blame her. I'm not so sure I wouldn't try the same thing under different circumstances.

As Katie leaves, others trickle into the conference room: a few folks from HR, our head of communications, and what looks to be most of our finance and legal teams. I'm relieved when I see a few more agents step in, including my good friend Naomi. She leads the TV division, and we started around the same time and bonded through the war that is signing talent in Hollywood.

As we take our seats, the head of strategy opens the meeting with an overview of why we are here. He highlights the steps of the regulatory process and what we need to accomplish by when. Besides the basics, they want to outline how we work: our priorities, strategy, goals, and processes, even the culture behind all of it.

Each agent shares a little about their area of expertise so Wyatt and the others can understand the agency's collaborative approach to representation. I go last, so there's not much more to add before I look back at Wyatt for next steps.

"I thought you focused on stories that are authentic and avoid positioning women's stereotypical feminine roles," Wyatt says, and all I can do is force a tight-lipped smile because I'm in shock. How does he know?

He shares a story about a script that was misogynistic and in service to the male leads and how I pushed the producers and writers to change it. The female lead isn't there to subscribe to old-fashioned gender roles. It doesn't reflect how women lead their lives in the real world today.

He thinks it's important to capture nuances in our services like that.

As he's talking, all I can see is the guy I fell for so many years ago. It makes me think about how we used to connect over our passion and dreams for the future. He knew all about my goal to become a lawyer and would list off all my accomplishments whenever I used to doubt myself.

"Did I get that right, Blair?"

I snap out of my daydream about what used to be and smile and nod. I'm not sure exactly what he was saying, but I think it was more cheerleading on my behalf.

"Of course. Thank you for the kind words, Wyatt."

I look around the room to see if anyone notices how awkward and uncomfortable I am. The only person who seems to notice anything is Naomi. She has one eyebrow raised as if to say, *Who is the president of your fan club, girl?*

Naomi walks up after the meeting ends and introduces herself to Wyatt. "So, how do you two know each other?" she asks.

"Blair and I grew up together," Wyatt answers before I can respond.

"We went to the same high school," I interject.

Naomi looks like she's just solved the *New York Times* crossword puzzle. "So, you two have history."

"If by history you mean we knew each other," I stammer while trying to act unaffected. I don't think I'm pulling it off at all. I look over at Wyatt, and he looks...hurt?

"But, you're friends now?" Naomi pushes.

"Strictly professional," I say smugly as I flash my best "fuck you" grin at Wyatt, making sure he knows I got his message loud and clear.

I feel vindicated, but the look on his face squeezes my heart. I shake my head to myself because this is ridiculous. What we had was a stupid teenage fling where I was silly enough to think he was my one true love. Spoiler: the first guy you sleep with is never your soulmate, no matter how it feels.

Ok, I need to get out of here. Let's wrap up this meeting because being around Wyatt is causing me to have some feelings that need to stay buried. There's no way I'm going back there, and he's made it clear he's not interested.

I need to figure out how to minimize my time on this task force. I don't even represent his sister yet, so other than the occasional red carpet event or party, there is absolutely no reason for us to see each other.

"I better get back to my office," I say.

I hug Naomi and promise to meet for lunch soon and then give a small wave to Wyatt. I see Katie has returned and is eager to escort him to his next meeting. When I turn back to sneak a look at him, his eyes are on me, and they look anything but professional.

sixteen

. . .

WYATT

"I HEAR you've been spending time with a certain talent agent," Jake says with a smirk as he walks into my office and relaxes on the couch that sits along a wall of windows looking out over the LA Westside. "Is she as professional as you hoped?"

For all the confidentiality surrounding lawyers, they sure are the biggest gossips. No doubt he heard about the meetings at TWA from one of the attorneys over there. I know Jake is giving me shit. He's convinced this is one of those second-chance romance setups his soon-to-be wife is always reading about.

"I've only been in one meeting with her this week, and I'm not even sure how many more will be necessary. It shouldn't take long for her to summarize how things work from an agent's point of view."

It's true, but technically, I don't need to spend any additional time with Blair, either. She could simply let the in-house legal team know, or we could correspond via email.

Instead, I've had our team here set up a series of meetings daily because I want to guarantee I run into her.

"Well then, I suppose that's good."

Jake lies back on the couch, getting comfortable.

"Get your shoes off that couch," I snap.

Jake adjusts so his feet are hanging over the couch's arm.

I get up and walk over to the coffee bar opposite the couch and grab us both a cup. If he's stretching out, he'll be here for a minute, and I might as well take a break.

"So, why are you here?" I ask.

"Final tux fitting. Thought maybe you'd want to come along and see how yours fits, too."

As the best man, I should be more on top of all this, but clearly, I've been distracted.

"Sorry, man. Of course, I'll go with."

"I didn't come here to guilt you, but since we're on the topic of guilt, any more thoughts about coming over to Hays and Cole?"

That's the firm where Jake has been since we graduated. The best entertainment law firm in LA—and where I would work if I weren't expected to fulfill a legacy.

"Come on, man. You know I think about it all the time. But it's never going to happen. I appreciate you still holding out hope."

"Ryan wants to meet with you."

What? Ryan Cole is one of the founders and one of LA's most successful and influential lawyers. I am absolutely stunned. This is the firm I once dreamed of working for, the place where my aspirations of shaping the entertainment industry felt most possible. I've always been trapped by this deep sense of loyalty to my father, and the thought of leaving his practice feels like a betrayal. I'm not sure I could do it.

I allow myself to daydream for a minute about the opportunity to learn from the best in the business, someone whose work I've admired for so long. I could meet with him. It doesn't have to mean anything. Networking is important in our field.

"Oh, yeah? About what?"

"You know fucking what."

"I'm sure he's just heard I'm working on the TWA merger and it's just a pleasant opportunity to network." I try to act like this isn't a big deal by sitting back down and pretending to look at something important on my computer.

"Whatever you need to tell yourself, Wyatt. Just call his office and set something up. Sooner rather than later."

"Thanks, man."

Jake and I spend the lunch hour together, but I can't seem to concentrate once I'm back in the office.

I can't stop thinking about Blair. More specifically, I can't stop thinking about how much she believed in me and how her support made me feel invincible. I hate how I feel so resigned to my career, as opposed to the hope I once felt when I was with her. It wouldn't surprise her that Ryan Cole wanted to meet with me. Why am I so surprised by it?

My father made a convincing argument that I was being led by lust and I couldn't trust an eighteen-year-old girl to guide my decisions around my future.

His logic made sense, and I took his advice to take a break from spending time with her so I could get my thoughts in order. In hindsight, it was foolish to think I could take a pause while I figured things out and she would just be ok with no contact and wait for me. She ended up going to prom with her neighbor, Justin. They'd been friends forever, but I know he always hoped there would be more. I ended up going with Holly, but just as friends.

I stopped by her house after graduation, but she was out with her friends. I never got the nerve to talk to her again before I left for college. I wanted to. It's probably the only time I was close to being in love with someone, not that I even know what that feels like. But I can tell you I've never felt that way about another woman since her. When I saw the tabloids of her with that reality star, I knew that I'd missed my chance.

I open my laptop and type her name in the search bar. I wonder why she kept the name Bennett. Does she still love him? The search pulls up images of her with Billy. I would be jealous, but he looks like a total douche, and in almost every photo, she looks fake. She's smiling, but she doesn't look like she's in love. I don't know what's wrong with me that I'm thrilled at the idea she may have been unhappy with him.

I see a few more articles about deals she signed. She really is single-handedly paving the way for more women to have bigger roles in Hollywood. Her last three films centered on female leads, writers, and directors. All had top box-office numbers for their premiere weekend. She's placed more female directors on projects than any other agency.

One journalist is following her work and has a story about how much revenue Blair's brought into TWA by focusing on women. She's speculating that in the next two years, the agency could earn most of its money from women-centered projects. It's quite impressive.

I'm about to click out of this rabbit hole before I reach stalker level when I see a news link promoting her at the Paley Center tomorrow night.

Paley Center presents A Conversation with Blair Bennett, The Wynn Agency, and Jess Lexington, Editor-In-Chief – On the Red Carpet. Join Blair and Jess as they discuss whether there are enough complex roles for women and when we might reach that invisible tipping point.

I click into the event and purchase a ticket. Now that I've seen her again, I'll do anything to spend more time with or around her.

Maybe Jake is right about second chances.

seventeen

. . .

BLAIR

"THE IDEA there aren't enough roles for complex women is ridiculous. On average, the Writers Guild receives about fifty thousand scripts a year, but we're only making anywhere from a hundred to a hundred and fifty. We need a better process for finding those scripts."

The conversation with Jess is going well. I don't mind speaking in public. I'm passionate about this topic, and it's great publicity for the agency. I know I've proven myself, but it's a cutthroat world, so it never hurts to stay top of mind.

"Do we have enough women working in Hollywood to make this change?" Jess asks me.

"We have enough to make a difference, but we could always use more. I always loved what the late great Ruth Bader Ginsburg used to say: 'We'll have enough women on the Supreme Court when there are nine.'" I glance out into the cheering audience, and that's when I see him.

What is he doing here?

I turn back to Jess to refocus.

"Women write just over thirty percent of all scripts and make only a quarter of all movies and TV," I say. "Changing those percentages is simple. We just need to choose scripts written by women. Find female cinematographers and editors. Find females to exec produce and direct."

"You make it sound so easy," Jess says, trying to lighten the conversation, and the crowd chuckles. She's setting me up so I can bring it home.

I smile along because this is the part that drives me crazy.

"Honestly, Jess, it is. You just have to pick through the stack of submissions and find the stories. They are out there. We've made significant progress in hiring practices at many agencies. Women make up almost forty percent of agents in town. We can make this happen if we want to."

I look back at the audience and see Wyatt with an expression of pride on his face. His attention is latched on me, and I know that smile. It's the same way he used to look at me any time I won a debate or was passionate about a particular topic. He made me feel special, like my ideas and opinions mattered. I've missed that feeling.

"Thank you, Blair," says Jess. "Thank you for being such an inspiration and making it your mission to advocate to see more women in front of and behind the camera. I know, with you leading the charge, Hollywood is going to change for the better."

Jess says a few more things to the crowd, but my eyes are on Wyatt as he gets up from his seat and walks out the back door. I'm surprised when my heart drops a bit, and I realize that I was hoping to talk to him.

As I exit the stage, I spot Grant and make my way over to

my studio exec friend. I'm encouraged that he's here for this topic.

"Ms. Bennett, always nice to see you out advocating for women," Grant says as he raises his glass in a toast and then brings it to his lips.

"Someone has to," I reply.

"Oh, come on, Blair. You know I support your efforts in this space. I just don't get pitched that many opportunities to do so. Do you have anything good for me yet?"

I know he's taunting me because he's not wrong. He can only support what he's presented, and as much as studios promote and advocate for more diversity in Hollywood, they are only half of the problem—or solution.

"I will soon. You know I'm working on some interesting changes to my roster."

He knows I'm hoping to sign Sophia. Until I do, I need to make more time for him so it's easier to pitch my projects. Almost everything he touches turns into a box office hit or critical success, and it would be amazing to work more with Wonderland Studios. They have the most talent-friendly reputation in the industry, thanks to him.

"Anytime, Blair. You know I'll always make time for you." As he reaches out to touch my arm, I feel another arm come around my waist. I look to my left and see Wyatt standing so close that I can see his jaw twitch as he smiles at Grant. I'm distracted by how good he smells, like cedarwood and leather, with a hint of ocean.

"Nice to see you again, Greg."

Grant has a knowing grin on his face as he shakes Wyatt's hand. "It's Grant." He knows Wyatt knows his name.

Everyone knows Grant's name. "Nice to see you two together again."

I step away from Wyatt and give him my best professional glare that says, please don't embarrass me, but also, please make a good impression on the most respected studio executive in town.

"Oh, no, Wyatt and I are just acquaintances. Sophia. Brother. Nothing more."

Grant looks between us, and a slight grin creeps over his face.

"I remember. I'm one of Sophia's biggest fans. She's very talented," he says, slipping back into his professional demeanor. "Blair, I'll let you go, but lunch soon. Next week, if you can?"

Wyatt and I say goodbye to Grant. As soon as he's out of earshot, I turn to Wyatt, frustrated that he gets me so flustered.

"What are you doing here?" I look at him, but his eyes are focused on my lips. I remember his full, soft lips kissing me for the first time and how he would always tuck my hair behind my ears before leaning his forehead against mine.

"I wanted to see you in action." He steps closer to me like he knows he could have me if he wanted.

"So, this is a professional visit?"

"Sure."

"Your arm around my waist didn't feel professional."

"Good."

He's managed to back me against the wall. I put my hands up on his chest to push him back, but he grabs my hands and holds them there. His top two buttons are open, and I can see the light spattering of hair on his sculpted chest. My hands twitch with the need to feel him. He's staring at me with a longing in his eyes, but I know better than to trust that look. It's the same one he had back then. Like we were meant to be.

I want to tell him how much he hurt me. I want to ask him what happened. There's still a part of me that believes everything we shared, our connection, was real. I'm desperate for there to be an explanation or excuse, but I know better. That's just my idealistic thinking.

I snap back to reality and gently push him away from me.

"I need to get back out there."

As I turn to walk away, Jess races up to me and pulls me into a hug. "Babe, you were fucking fire up there!"

Wyatt steps back, but Jess sees him and looks at us with wonder on her face.

"Jess, this is Wyatt. Wyatt, this is my best friend, Jess."

Her eyes grow big as she looks at me again. A huge grin escapes from her lips, and she puts her hand out to greet Wyatt. "Wyatt, so nice to finally meet you. I've heard so much."

Mortified, I close my eyes. I don't need him to think that I talk about him at all.

"Really," he said, looking pointedly at me with a smirk on his face. "Wish I could say the same, but it's still a pleasure to meet anyone who's close to Blair." He's pulling out all the charm.

"It would be hard to tell you anything since we don't talk," I snip at him.

Jess pulls us both over to the bar so she can fill us in on

the gossip she's heard from socializing around the room this evening. She and Wyatt seem to hit it off and somehow become best friends. I vow to kill her once I get her alone. She should know better than to fraternize with the enemy.

As the room clears, I wrap up my last conversations and officially call it a night.

"You ready?" I ask Jess, and she turns and gives me a look I already don't like.

"Wyatt, is there any chance you can take Blair home? She rode with me, but I need to run by the office to finish up a story I'm on deadline for."

I will kill her. I'm going to end up in jail for killing my best friend. Who knew it would end this way?

"Of course. I'm happy to give Blair a ride," he says with way too much innuendo, and he and Jess lock eyes with amusement. They are no longer allowed to hang out with each other if they aim to torture me.

"Let's go," I say to Wyatt. "And you are dead to me," I whisper to Jess.

She laughs as she hugs me and then whispers in my ear, "You're welcome."

eighteen

. . .

WYATT

I HOLD the passenger door open and offer my hand to help Blair into my car. She looks fucking incredible. She always does. Tonight, she's in a black suit and five-inch Christian Louboutin heels that bring her close to my height. It took all my willpower not to look at her chest since she wasn't wearing a shirt under that suit jacket. I felt both anxious and hopeful about the possibility of a wardrobe malfunction, but obviously, she knows what she's doing.

Her hair is blown out with thick, dark waves that drop past her shoulders and down to the middle of her back. Her eyes pop, an almost translucent honey color, and those lips...

Jesus, save me.

There's a gloss on them with a hint of neutral color, just the right amount that I could kiss her and it wouldn't mess up her makeup.

She slides into my car with ease, and something about it feels right. Like she belongs in that seat. Belongs with me. I allow myself a moment to imagine she's coming home with me, and desire makes my heart ache. What was I thinking when I suggested we stay professional? I was trying to be respectful of what I thought she wanted, but I don't want that. And I don't want her to think that I want that.

I'm still in my head when she breaks the silence.

"Why did you get back together with Holly?" Her stare is focused on the city lights zipping by her passenger window. When I don't answer immediately, she turns her head and gives me a determined look. "You said all those things, Wyatt. I believed you. I thought..." She cuts herself off and returns her gaze to the lights flying by. "Never mind. It doesn't even matter anymore."

I rub my forehead and then down my face as I take in and release a deep breath. At some point, we need to talk about this if there's to be any chance of moving past it.

"I didn't want to. We didn't really..." I try to find exactly how to tell her I was a coward and that I hate how much control my father has—or had—over my decisions.

Her eyebrows pull together, and she tilts her head at me in disbelief. Her eye contact game is strong.

"Our parents became close. When Holly and I broke up, it was awkward at first when our families spent time together, but they seemed to accept it." I stop talking for a minute. I don't want this to reopen any wounds. I clear my throat.

"Holly and her parents were over for dinner, and my father brought up prom. I knew my dad leveraged the fact that we were dating to manage some business deals with her dad. I'm not sure if Holly said something to her parents or if there were other factors, but it was clear his expectation was I would take Holly to prom as originally planned."

Just saying it out loud makes me feel foolish.

"I didn't know how to tell you. I hated my dad. I hated myself. I kind of just checked out after that and went into zombie mode."

I don't tell Blair that my dad blamed her for my lack of focus, that he claimed she was distracting me and would ruin everything I had worked so hard for.

"Then you went to prom with Justin, but by then, I knew I'd fucked up by not being honest with you. I knew you hated me by then."

"Wyatt, I've had a crush on you since I was sixteen years old, the first time I saw you at the golf course."

I flinch at her declaration and shake my head. "What? You are the one who pushed me to go out with Holly."

"I know. I was a total coward. But in my defense, you also looked at her like you were undressing her with your eyes."

The car is quiet while I try to make sense of this confession. She rests her head against the seat as she watches me, but I can tell there's more she wants to say. Her hand runs back and forth along the chain around her neck. It's something she's always done before she speaks up.

"Truth?" she says, holding on to that chain but still faces me.

"Always the truth," I tell her as I reach for her hand in her lap. She's invoking the phrase equivalent of the pinky swear. We would say this to each other in high school when we wanted total honesty, no judgement. When she intertwines her fingers with mine, I feel a level of comfort I haven't experienced since I was last with her.

"I know we were young, but you were my entire world. I

was so invested in being part of your orbit, but I would get crushed by the smallest hints of rejection, so I didn't risk telling you how I felt."

"What rejection?" I ask.

"If I asked if you wanted to come over and you said you had to work, I immediately felt devastated and assumed it was because I wasn't enough for you. I know it sounds ridiculous now. The thought of sharing my feelings with you was terrifying. I couldn't risk the idea of not having you in my life, so I wouldn't do anything to disrupt our friendship."

"But you are the one who kissed me." I look at her, still shocked by her confession.

"I know. When you broke up with Holly, it felt like a do-over. We were spending even more time together, confiding in each other, getting closer. I don't know where the confidence came from. It was a total fluke."

She bites her lip, nervously waiting for me to respond. I want to savor this moment. It feels like she could forgive me. Like she wants to forgive me.

I park in front of her house, and before she reaches for the door, I try to keep us in the moment for a little longer.

"Truth?" I ask her.

"Always the truth."

"I've had a crush on you since the moment I met you. Being around you was so easy and fun. I knew the first time we kissed that I had messed up. That I had wasted all that time with Holly when I should have been dating you."

I reach for her other hand and lace my fingers through hers. Hope rises in my chest.

For a moment, we are back in those feelings. She's gazing

at me like she's remembering everything that happened that spring.

I lean in slowly so I don't scare her away and barely brush my lips on hers. "I'm going to kiss you now, ok?"

She tilts her head in a slight nod, and I press my lips against hers before she can change her mind. I've been waiting to taste her since the minute I saw her in Sophia's trailer.

She brings her hand up to my cheek, and I take that as permission to gently slide my tongue across the seam of her lips. I slip into her mouth and swirl my tongue with hers. She greets me with the same energy, but it instantly turns more eager.

I bring both my hands to her jaw and slide them into her hair, and when a slight moan escapes from her mouth, I'm instantly hard.

We move in closer, trying to connect our bodies the best we can in the front seat of this car. I want to pull her over to straddle my lap, but I don't want to spook her, and I don't want this kiss to end yet.

She breaks the kiss for a moment to whisper my name and then pulls my lips back to hers with force, pushing her tongue into mine like she's desperate.

I am so desperate.

Desperate to touch her, taste her, feel inside of her.

I move my right hand down her neck and to her collarbone, and the touch breaks the trance we are in.

Blair pulls back, her eyes wide like she's surprised, but she doesn't panic. She takes her hand from mine and rests her first and second fingers on her lips, like she is cherishing the touch of my lips on hers and committing it to memory.

"I'm going to go. Thank you for the ride home, Wyatt."

My hands gently slide down her arms and away from her as she moves to open the door.

"Wait. Let me get the door."

I jump out and adjust myself quickly before I run around the car. After opening her door, I reach in and help her step out of the car.

"Goodnight, Blair." I place my hands on her hips and slide close, risking it for one more small kiss. She doesn't push me away, and I'm addicted.

She walks into her house, and I wait until the door is closed before I lean back against my car, press the palms of my hands to my eyes, and sigh.

nineteen

. . .

BLAIR

"HERE, TRY SOME OF THIS," Stella says as she hands me a jar of lip mask treatment. I snap out of my daze and stare at her.

I must look confused because she says, "You keep touching your lips, so I thought maybe you needed something for them?"

"Oh. Yes, thank you."

I can't tell her I keep touching my lips because I keep thinking about Wyatt's lips on them last night.

I can't believe I kissed him. I can't believe how good that kiss was. I thought I had over-inflated my memory of his kiss because it seemed unlikely that the best kiss of my life would be with an eighteen-year-old boy. I was wrong. It was. Well, until last night. Now that is the new bar.

He broke my heart. I swore I would never forgive him. However, I also didn't think I'd ever see him again once we graduated, so I relented and did my best to move on. Is it wrong that I feel better knowing he didn't want to get back with Holly?

Don't judge me. I know Holly was my friend, but she wasn't the poster child for committed relationships. It was obvious she didn't want to be with Wyatt toward the end. For the record, when he confirmed he didn't have feelings for her, I confessed to Holly that I liked him. She told me to go for it.

Oddly, I understood his need to please his parents. I was an only child to parents who'd had me later in life. The expectations and delusion around my perfection were off the charts.

It's funny what stories you'll tell yourself when you don't have all the facts. I wish he would've trusted me enough to understand the pressure he was under, but it sounds like he just shut down. I wonder if that is why he stuck with his original UCLA plans.

"Grant confirmed lunch for tomorrow, too," Stella says. "I've booked you at The Ivy."

I pull my head out of memory lane and stare at her in shock. "I can't believe he's available to meet with me so quickly—this is wild." I shake my head. I'm used to booking so far ahead that you forget why you're trying to meet with someone by the time you actually get to meet.

"He asked a lot of questions about Sophia. He seemed eager to talk about what projects she's working on." Stella says this like it's not the most unusual thing to ever happen.

"You spoke with Grant directly? Not his assistant?"

"No, he called directly to set it up. Was that not ok?" she asks with a worried frown.

I reassure her that she did nothing wrong and explain that it's not typical for execs to book their own calendars—mostly because they probably don't even know what is on their calendars half the time.

I'm suspicious about why Grant is so interested in Sophia. I haven't signed her yet. I wonder if he's heard something that could help or hurt. You never know which way it will go in this town.

It could be a good play to invite her along. I have nothing specific to pitch to Grant yet, but it's always good to keep him close. He may know of a few things, too. I grab my phone and pull up the last text exchange I had with Sophia.

ME

Any chance you are available for lunch tomorrow? Before you answer, I'm asking you if you want to have lunch with me and Grant Hall.

SOPHIA

Seriously? YES! Tell me where and when.

ME

I'll have Stella send over the details. I'll pick you up and we can brief on the way there.

SOPHIA

Fantastic. Thank you!

I heart her comment and set the phone down. Moments later, as I'm trying to focus on work, my phone buzzes again.

WYATT

Hi. How's your day going?

I notice I touch my lips again and immediately get butter-flies in my stomach.

I'm so fucked.

Something has shifted since we talked about what happened. It felt good to be honest with him. It felt good to kiss him, too, but that cannot happen again. I'm trying to sign his sister, and we're working on the merger project together—not to mention his firm stance a few weeks ago when he was adamant about keeping things professional.

ME

Busy.

WYATT

Can I take you to lunch tomorrow?

ME

Can't. Already have plans.

WYATT

🙂 Is that an excuse?

ME

No, meeting with Grant to talk about some projects.

I see the three dots in a bubble pop up, disappear, pop up, disappear like he wants to say something but is struggling with what to say.

He's still convinced there may be "hidden feelings" between me and Grant. I could correct him easily, but I'm having a little too much fun.

WYATT

Where are you guys going for lunch?

ME

I'm not sure yet. We thought we'd play it by ear.

WYATT

I was just going to offer some recommendations if you didn't have a place yet.

I don't tell him his sister is joining us. It's good for him to squirm a bit.

ME

Sure you were.

WYATT

A guy can't even help a friend out anymore. Wow.

Is that what we are? *Friends?* My heart drops when I see that in his text. I don't like how that sounds.

ME

Ha, ha, FRIEND. Appreciate the offer. All good here.

As soon as I send the text, I immediately regret writing FRIEND in all caps. It looks passive aggressive. And it sounds like I'm mad now and blowing him off. Ugh. This is why I don't text back immediately. I need a minute to compose responses.

WYATT

Raincheck?

ME

Sure.

I let out a sigh of relief that he didn't seem bothered by my response. And as much as I hate the sound of *friend* coming from him, right now, it's really all I'm able to offer him, too.

twenty

. . .

BLAIR

"I NEED to confess that I have a small crush on Grant Hall," Sophia tells me as she gets into my car.

"Please don't tell him that. He doesn't need any more women to feed his ego!" I joke with her.

She looks at me, her brows knit with worry. "Is he a jerk?"

"No, no, I was kidding. He's actually one of the nicest guys in Hollywood. He's tough. He takes his job seriously and has a bit of a reputation for being a hard-ass, depending on who you ask."

I give her the background on how he rose through the ranks and is a bit of a box-office whisperer. In an industry that is competing with technology giants and using data to get ahead, Grant is someone who believes in following his gut vs. following data. He has an exceptional ability to understand and read people and an even better aptitude for what audiences and fans want.

"I sound terrible," Sophia says. "I don't mean to demean his talent and make it about his looks, but the guy is so hot!"

I throw my head back and laugh. It is so refreshing to see someone as talented as she is, and currently in the biggest spotlight there is, act like a normal twenty-something with a crush.

Celebrities. They're just like us.

"He's definitely what some would refer to as a DILF."

"He's a dad?" Sophia snaps to look at me, her shock apparent.

"Yeah, and if you think he's charming now, just wait until he brings his daughter to an event. Any woman in the vicinity will feel her ovaries melt."

"Oh, so is he with someone, then?" I catch a flicker of disappointment in her eyes.

"No, and that is the big mystery. Geneva is the mother, but she's not in the picture at all."

"The supermodel?" Sophia asks. "That child must be gorgeous."

"Yeah, they were an item for a hot minute a few years ago. He has full custody, though. I don't know the story there. No one does. He's very private about his personal life."

"Hmm." Sophia pinches her lips between her fingers as she looks out the passenger window. "He must be. I sat next to him all night at *Pink Slip*, and he never mentioned he had a daughter."

I shift topics and let her know this isn't a big pitch but more of a relationship-building opportunity. Part of Grant's process of knowing if a project is going to work is also about the people. He's meticulous in understanding the personalities of talent and creators, and he works hard to pull together a team that connects as well off the screen as they do on screen. There's a reason everyone wants to work with him and his team at Wonderland Studios.

"Just be yourself. He'll want to get to know Sophia the person, not necessarily Sophia the actress."

She nods and tells me how refreshing that is to hear.

Because she's still so young, it's easy to forget that she's been in this industry for so long. You'd think, since most of her work was on a TV series or original movies for kid channels, that she was protected from some of the darker politics in Hollywood, but you'd be wrong. Some of the worst corruption happens to young actors just starting out. It's easy for studios to take advantage of fresh talent who might not realize what they can negotiate. This business is so competitive, and if you've made it, you don't want to fail. Sometimes, that means you adjust your personality to do whatever it takes, even if what it takes is not in alignment with your values or morals.

From conversations we've had, I know Sophia was lucky and most of her experience was fantastic, but there were a few incidents where things could have gone terribly wrong.

I look nervously over at Sophia. I hope I don't piss her off with what I'm about to share.

"I may have shared that I'm hoping to sign you. I hope that is ok. I've not talked about any projects yet, either. I think if we can focus on what you are interested in, ideal roles, it will ensure you are top of mind in the event those roles are ever pitched to him, regardless of who represents you."

Even though a lot of projects pitched to studios have

people attached to produce, direct, or act, a studio can always influence the final decision.

"It's absolutely ok. I don't think it has to be a secret that we're talking."

When we arrive at The Ivy, Grant is already waiting for us, and I glance at my watch to see if we are late. We're actually early, so I'm relieved but surprised that he beat us here. He must really be interested in catching up.

After hugs, kisses, and reintroductions, I'm surprised when Grant starts the conversation.

"You absolutely deserved the Oscar. It was by far the best performance of the year."

Sophia immediately blushes, and I know she must be dying a little on the inside to receive such a big compliment from Grant.

"Thank you. That means a lot coming from you." Their eyes lock and linger a bit, and suddenly, I feel like a third wheel at this lunch.

I wonder if I'm reading the vibes right when Grant snaps out of his trance and immediately gets the conversation back on track by asking Sophia to tell him how she got started in this business.

The hour goes by quickly, and before I have a chance to tell him about some scripts on my desk, he gets an alert that he's needed back at the office. I'm a little disappointed, but overall, it was a big win because it appears he and Sophia had a great connection. Without a doubt, she won him over, and I know that she'll be on the roster of talent he likes to work with.

"Blair, I'm sorry we didn't talk more about your projects,

but it's obvious we'll be talking more about the talent you're collecting. I'll be seeing you again soon." He's not even looking at me when he says this. There's definitely a vibe happening here.

I nod in agreement. I don't want to disrupt the mood. As he stands, he hesitates a minute before leaving the table. He walks away but turns back quickly.

"I'd like to invite the both of you out to my summer party in the Hamptons. I'll have my assistant send over the details to Stella."

I nod again because I'm speechless. In all my years at TWA, I have never made the invite list to a Grant Hall summer party. It is beyond exclusive.

"Did he just..." Sophia doesn't even finish. She's just as shocked as I am.

"You must have really impressed him!" I tell her. I don't add that I think he may also have a crush on her, too.

Just then, my phone buzzes, and when I look down to see who it is, Sophia notices Wyatt's name on the screen.

WYATT

How's lunch?

"Why is he asking about this lunch? Did you tell him we were meeting Grant?"

Is she mad? Should I have mentioned it to him? I'm not exactly sure how to tell her that Wyatt knows I had lunch plans with Grant because he asked me to lunch, but I led him to believe I was meeting with Grant alone so I could be funny and evil and make him jealous instead of telling him I was bringing his sister.

"No, I'm not sure. I guess it's just lunchtime. You know your brother is weird."

I hold my breath, hoping she buys that excuse. It's another reminder of why we won't work as anything more than colleagues. It would be so awkward.

"He totally is. I know you have history, but don't let him bother you. He can be overbearing and protective of me. I appreciate it, but it can become a bit much sometimes."

I leave him on read just to mess with him.

As we walk to the car, she looks over at me like she wants to ask me more about our history.

"He's not bothering me. And I know you want to ask. Go ahead."

When we get into the car, she fires off about twenty questions in one breath: "How did you meet? Was it love at first sight? How long were you together? Why did you break up?"

It's that last one that sticks with me.

"The short version is he was dating my friend Holly and, when they broke up, we sort of started dating. And then he started dating her again but failed to let me know."

"He didn't," she whispers.

"Yeah, I found out when she told me they were going to prom together."

I spare her the details of him taking my virginity.

I confess to her that we did finally talk about it the other night and that he explained how her dad and Holly's parents concocted the reunion. She tells me that what they did was bullshit, upset with her parents in my defense, but I tell her I understand what it's like to want to please your parents.

"I vaguely remember some of this," she says. "Not the

details, but I remember Wyatt was so angry when we were moving him into UCLA. He refused to talk to our dad the entire summer. I'm not even sure when they started talking again. Just one day, he was over it, I guess."

I want to ask her more questions about Wyatt. Did he mention me or seem sad? I push down my curiosity and tell her it was just young love. I'm glad Wyatt told me what happened, but it was all so long ago. I'm just glad we can be friends.

"You know, this sounds like the start of a Hollywood rom-com. Maybe we pitch this to Grant next year," she says with a glint of hope in her eye.

I laugh at Sophia's romantic idealism and try to tell her that the ending would make it a tragedy, but she looks directly at me and says, "The story isn't over. I just know it."

I swallow hard and don't say a word because something deep down wants her to be right.

twenty-one

. . .

WYATT

BLAIR LEFT me on read on purpose. She knows what she's doing. I can't focus on anything at work right now, so I decide to head over to Sophia's house. I'm curious if she's met with Blair again about representing her.

When I pull up to Sophia's place, there's a car I don't recognize in the driveway. I knock instead of using my key so that I don't walk into something I'm not prepared to see.

When Sophia opens the door, she gives me an enormous hug, and I squeeze her back. There is nothing better in this world than hugs from my sister.

"We were just talking about you!" she tells me as she steps back to welcome me inside.

"Who's we?" I ask, and then Blair walks around the corner.

My heart beats wildly, and I immediately scan her body. She's so beautiful that it takes my breath away. She's wearing cream-colored pants that are cropped at the ankle, showing off another pair of Louboutin heels. They're not as tall this time, but they are still incredibly sexy on her. I immediately wonder what she looks like in nothing but those heels.

My eyes continue up her body, coming to rest on a silky beige top that crosses and drapes along her breasts in a way that makes them the star of the show. All I want to do is put my mouth on those breasts. They would perfectly fill my hands. They look like they are still real, which is rare around here. As my eyes finish the journey up her body, I catch her glaring at me.

Busted.

She's smirking with her eyes slightly squinted, like she's suspicious of why I'm here. I swear I didn't know she would be here.

"What are you doing here?" I ask her.

"We had lunch with Grant Hall!" my sister says, twirling once. As she heads into the kitchen, she asks us what we want to drink.

"Oh, I didn't know you were having lunch with Grant today." I glare at Blair. She failed to tell me my sister would be with her.

Blair blushes and bites her lower lip. She knows she's guilty but doesn't look bothered by the omission one bit.

"It was amazing, Wy... He asked me so many questions, and he listened to everything I was telling him. It was surprising, really." She says this as if he's the only one who's ever really listened to her before. I sneak a look at Blair and tilt my head in question. She just shrugs like it's no big deal.

But then my sister drops the news about the invite to his end-of-summer party. That is a big deal. It's one of the most exclusive parties in entertainment.

"Wow, sis, that's amazing." I reach out for a hug while trying to casually see if Blair is going. "He invited both of you?"

"I'm sure I was only invited because it would've been rude to only invite your sister in front of me," she says as she laughs at the idea of the invite.

"You've never been before?" I ask Blair.

"No. Never."

Dread sets in. He must be trying to make his move on Blair, then. I know they are close. They both claim to be only friends, but they also seem to go to a lot of premiere events together, too. Now he's inviting her into his inner circle. He wants her closer to him. I can't compete with that. I need more time with her. I need to remind her of how good we are together. Or how good we could be. And I need him to fuck off and flirt with someone else. Blair is off limits.

"I have an invite for you, too," I blurt out. "Join me as my plus-one for Jake's wedding." It's so out of context that I'm immediately mortified and want to retract the invite. Sophia looks back and forth between us with a look of confusion and surprise, but to her credit, she quickly adapts to the abrupt change of topic.

"You absolutely should. Then I wouldn't have to sit on the groom's side alone," she says, and I silently thank her for trying to save me before I backtrack a bit.

"I mean, you might have plans. It's ok if you do."

Now Sophia is looking at me like I've grown two heads, and I'm kicking myself for how impulsive I am whenever I'm around Blair.

"Do I know Jake?" she asks with a confused frown.

"He's my best friend. Roommate from college. I'm the best man. The reason you'd be sitting with Sophia." I shove my hands in my pocket to stop myself from fidgeting.

"And when is this wedding?"

"Yeah, sorry. It's July 4. Out in Santa Monica. Lauren, Jake's bride-to-be, wanted the fireworks to serve as the background for the event."

Sophia's phone rings, saving me from this completely mortifying invitation gone wrong.

"I've got to take this, but let me know if you decide to go to the wedding. I'm not kidding when I say I'd love to have a familiar face to sit with," Sophia says before she disappears.

Blair nods and tells her she's got to get back to the office and will catch up with her soon. I follow her to the door, and when she tries to open it, I stand close behind her and raise my hand to shut it.

"What are you doing?" She turns to face me, and I cage her in by placing my other hand on the door. Her chest rises as her breath gets faster.

"Were you trying to make me jealous when you left out the detail about my sister joining you for lunch?"

"I have no idea what you're talking about." Her gaze dips to my mouth, and I know she wants to kiss me again.

As my body brushes hers, her breasts press into my chest, and when I lean in to whisper in her left ear, she angles her head to give me more access.

"I think you do." I press into her more. I want her to feel what she's doing to me. She tilts her hips into me as a breath of air escapes from her lips. I'm not sure she realizes that she's reacting to me. I pull down my right hand and trace my fingers down her jawline and then her neck and across her collarbone. The breath that escapes her is filled with excitement and anticipation. My fingertips graze the swell of her breasts.

"Why did you invite me to your friend's wedding?"

"I figured you'd like spending more time with Sophia." I'm lying, and she knows it, too.

"I thought you wanted to keep things professional."

Fuck. I knew that was going to haunt me.

"Truth?"

"Always the truth."

"I lied."

She closes her eyes and leans her head back against the door as a sigh escapes. That little sound almost does me in, and it takes all of my restraint to push away from her.

"Have lunch with me tomorrow."

She breaks out of the moment. Clearing her throat, she adjusts her shirt and smooths it out. "You'll have to call Stella to see what's available."

Blair offers me her most professional smile, and God, if I don't love that sass she throws me. I take a moment to admire her incredible ass as she walks toward her car and then immediately wonder how the fuck I'm going to convince her to give me another chance.

twenty-two

. . .

BLAIR

"**DID** someone order potato balls and guava strudel?" Jess sings as she slides into my office.

Stella pops up out of her chair to grab the boxes from Jess, squealing with excitement. "My favorite thing is when you come to visit us!"

"You only love me because I feed you," Jess jokes.

"That's not true! I mean, I love all the snacks, but I think you are an amazing person. You are beautiful and talented—"

"I'm just kidding, Stella. I know. It's ok!"

I'm not sure how Stella has kept her positive and inno-cent personality. She is a genuinely nice person, and that's rare in Hollywood. She would die if anyone thought she was using them.

But do not mistake her kindness for weakness. I once saw her block an actress from as many restaurants as she could after she was rude to the catering staff at one of our office parties.

"However, my treats are to serve as bribery to find out

why Blair was having lunch with Grant Hall and Sophia Ford yesterday. Grant Hall doesn't do lunch." Jess has a smirk on her face as she stuffs another potato ball into her mouth.

I should have known that she would have heard about lunch.

"Pics?" I ask her. She would know if the paps got any shots.

"Not that I know of. I was talking to Wonderland's head of PR when Grant's assistant came by to give him a heads up just in case the press called."

I fill her in on the lunch and admit it surprised me, too, when Grant scheduled lunch.

"You need to keep this to yourself, but I think he may have a little crush on Sophia."

Stella's and Jess's heads snap to face me, and they gasp.

"Grant doesn't date," Jess says.

"Do you think Sophia likes him?" Stella asks.

I nod. "She mentioned she thought he was attractive. But everyone thinks he's attractive, so hard to say." I share that regardless of attraction, they both seemed to hit it off and had some passionate conversations about filmmaking and discussing some of their old favorites.

"Speaking of Sophia...have you seen Wyatt?" Jess taunts.

"You mean other than the time you basically forced him to drive me home?" I roll my eyes. I haven't told anyone we kissed. I'm sure Jess is suspicious because I didn't follow up with her at all. Not even to yell at her.

"I just wondered if you two are staying close." She waggles her eyebrows and laughs.

"Ha, ha." I try to play it cool as I walk back to my desk. "I saw him yesterday when I dropped Sophia off at her house."

I shuffle through papers, avoiding eye contact, hoping to avoid this conversation. It will only bring back the feelings of him pressed against my body and how much I wanted him in that moment. His breath so close to my lips. Heat from his body against my thighs and stomach. Heat from my...

"You saw him yesterday?" Stella asks, interrupting my daydream. Her eyebrows are raised in surprise, or maybe she's a little hurt that I haven't mentioned it to her yet.

"You are so going to hook up," Jess says. "Stella, open your calendar. Let's get a pool going."

"We will not hook up," I say weakly. "He thinks Grant is after me, anyway."

"Why would he think that?" Stella wrinkles her nose, making the most innocent and confused face.

Jess throws her head back with a loud, hearty laugh. "The Paley Center event," she tells Stella. "Wyatt saw her talking to Grant, and his possessive instincts kicked in."

"They did not," I say. "And he was just saying hi."

"You went with him to *Pink Slip*, too," Stella chimes in. "It does seem a little sus."

"You never told me what happened on that ride home," Jess says. Both she and Stella are staring at me like they are waiting for story time.

I sigh and lean back in my chair. I might as well get this over with. Wyatt works from our TWA offices twice a week now, and it's just going to get harder to avoid seeing him. And the more I see him, the more I want to talk to him.

"I asked him why he got back together with Holly."

Both of my friends are staring at me wide-eyed, like they are afraid to push me for more details but are still dying to know the answer.

"His family has money. They ran in the same circles as Holly's parents. I guess they wanted Wyatt and Holly back together."

"And he didn't think to say no?" Jess asks. "How very arranged marriage of him."

In my next life, I want to be Jess. She is so confident and no-nonsense. She is always talking about how people over-complicate things and how she hates miscommunication. Though she's not a grudge holder, she doesn't have patience for people who won't step into their truth and take responsibility for their actions.

"I think he was just trying to please his parents. I know he gave up on golf because his dad had a different plan for him. It's not a stretch that his dad would control other parts of his life, too. But we didn't get that deep into the conversation."

In fact, my mind went straight to working out how I could justify forgiving what happened and what it might take to get over the pain he left behind. Maybe I was wrong to think he was all bad? We were so young.

I've been telling myself all this time that I must have misunderstood Wyatt's intentions, the way he wrapped his fingers kinto mine every time he was near me, how he always had to be touching me. We spent hours laying in the bed of his pickup, sharing stories about our dreams for the future. I told him about the pressure I sometimes felt being the only child. He shared how nervous he was about college. He didn't want to disappoint his father.

"He was my first," I tell Stella. Jess already knows.

"Oh, wow. They say you never forget your first," Stella says in almost a whisper.

It never felt like it was just about the sex. He was perfectly content to just spend time with me, which is why it fucked with my head so much that he seemed to just ditch me to go back to Holly. Did any of it mean anything to him? Was he that good of an actor? Was I totally delusional? Was I just not enough?

But it didn't matter if he was or wasn't into me. I was in love with him. Deeply. He was my first and only. I'm realizing he's likely been the bar for my future relationships—or lack of them.

I know I married Billy, but that was different. Billy was fun. He was the anti-depressant of boyfriends. He was great company and an even better distraction. But we both knew he didn't check all the boxes.

"So, what happens now?" Jess says, snapping me out of memory lane.

"Nothing. He's a professional colleague. And that's it." I take a bite of my guava strudel and lean back in my chair. I don't even believe it when I say it, and I can see both Jessica and Stella think I'm full of shit, too. Thankfully, the phone rings, saving me from having to say anything else.

"Oh, hi, Wyatt. Nice to hear from you." Stella's eyes are wide as she looks over at me and then back at Jess.

"Lunch? Oh, let me check." She puts the phone on mute and tells me he's calling to see if I'm available for lunch. Both ladies are quiet, waiting for me to say something. I want to see him again, but I don't think it's a good idea. The more time we spend together, the more I want to be around him, and that's a problem. It's weakening my resentment.

"Just book the lunch."

See how quickly I folded?

I get up from my desk and walk toward the bathroom.

"She's happy to join you today at noon. I'll put the details on her calendar. You have a good day, too." I know that running to the bathroom won't get me out of this conversation, but it will for now. As I shut the door, I hear Jessica yell, "I hope your legs are smooth and you are up to date on all your grooming!"

Oh, I definitely am.

twenty-three

. . .

WYATT

I'VE FINALLY CONVINCED Blair to have lunch with me on the days I work out of the TWA offices. She brought Stella along last week. I hoped it meant she didn't trust herself to be alone with me. But she's controlled herself just fine this week. Everything has been professional but friendly. It's been nice getting close to her again, but now I can't get her out of my head. She's playing the lead role in all of my shower scenes. I admit I'm looking for any excuse to spend time with her out of the office, even better if we're alone.

She still hasn't agreed to join me for Jake's wedding. It's a mind fuck that I'm desperate for her to say she'll go but also terrified she'll go. It's jumping right into dating vibes.

But she has a magnetic pull that I can't resist.

Maybe it's because we grew up together. Spending time with her was the best part of my day. When she asked me to be her first, my heart stopped. I wanted to be her first everything. I was already possessive, but this sealed that she would be mine forever.

The elevator door slides open, and I don't notice she's walking in behind me until I reach to press the button for our floor. I almost swallow my tongue. She's wearing a black dress that stretches around every single curve of her body like it's trying to hold on for dear life. I'm not sure how she got the dress on or, more importantly, how I could slide it off her. If I was curious about what she looked like under her clothes, I have a good idea now. The material stops mid-thigh, and her legs are bare all the way down to her black pointed heels. She taps her foot, and I snap my eyes back up to see her trying to hide a smirk.

Busted again.

"You look incredible."

I'm surprised to see her cheeks flush.

"Thank you."

"Not what I expected the dress code to be for a Monday morning."

I move closer to her as the doors close, crowding her against the back wall.

"Is that a good or bad thing?" she asks.

"Very good. Or maybe bad. Who did you put this dress on for?"

The chime of the elevator reaching our floor has us moving apart, but I'm not ready to end whatever connection we started behind closed doors. I hold my hand out so she can exit, and then I follow her, getting another perspective of the dress to admire.

"Stop looking at my ass," she says without looking back.

"I can't. It's literally perfection."

That gets a small huff of a laugh from her as she looks over her shoulder at me and rolls her eyes.

I follow her down the hall and into her office, surprising her when I shut the door behind me and lock it.

"What are you doing?" Her eyebrows make a V, and she looks irritated as she walks toward me. When she reaches past me to unlock the door, I grab her wrist.

"Wait."

She glares at me, hesitant about my intentions. I watch her look from my lips to my eyes and back to my lips again. Then I lean in a little closer, almost to her lips but not touching them. We're basically breathing into each other.

"Wyatt." She says my name like a plea, and I use it as permission to place my hands on her hips. Her hands grip my wrists as they move, but she doesn't stop me. I know I shouldn't be in here, but I can't resist. Every time I'm here, I'm forced to sit through meetings while watching her pull her hair over her shoulder and rub her hands down her neck—or bite her lip while she's reading documents.

It's not just her body or how she looks, though. She is fucking smart. She could run this agency. Every time we're in a meeting, the other departments continually defer to her for information or approval. She's been that way since I've known her: a natural leader and able to convince anyone to follow her.

I lean forward and dust my lips against hers. God, I love her lips. I take it slow to give her time to tell me what she wants. She takes in a breath and hesitates, not responding to me immediately, but then her hands slide up my arms, and she reaches around my neck. She presses her lips against mine, and I tilt my head for a better angle. My arms wrap around her, and I feel every part of her body against mine. I'm instantly hard, and when a small moan escapes her, I know she can feel me. My hands run across her curves and down her thighs, and I want nothing more than to reach under her dress. I'm obsessed with knowing if she still feels the same.

She runs the fingers from one hand through the short hairs at the base of my neck while dragging her other hand slowly across my chest, caressing each curve and dip like she's trying to memorize my body. I pull her leg up over mine and move my hand up the inside of her thigh until my thumb grazes her center.

"Yes," she whispers in my ear.

I run my thumb down the seam of her panties, and she is soaking wet. My dick was already hard, but now it's steel behind my zipper, desperate to be released.

I slide her underwear over to the side, and run my middle finger through her slit and slip inside her.

"Blair, is this all for me?"

Our stares still for a moment, and then she presses her mouth to mine, taking everything she wants from me. I feel her hands grabbing my hair and her nails drag my scalp. She's so fucking hot. I pull my focus back to her before I blow inside my pants.

"What do you need Blair? Tell me what you like."

"More," she whispers. "I need to feel more of you inside me."

I slide in another finger and pull my thumb up to circle

her bundle of nerves. The moan that escapes is loud and I bring my other hand up to cover her mouth.

"Quiet. I'm not sharing those sounds with anyone else."

Her head rolls back and I feel her breath gasping between my fingers. I twist my fingers to rub against that magic spot inside and she brings her head forward to mine, her hands gripping my neck like a vice.

I lean my head down and lick her neck, letting my teeth scrape up to her ear and then I whisper, "Come on Blair, come like a good girl for me."

It pushes her over the edge and I feel her body tense and release on my hand. I slow down, letting her catch her breath and the moment I remove my hand the door vibrates behind my back, echoing the deep sounds of knocking.

"Blair?" Stella says. "Sorry to interrupt, but it's ten a.m., and the meeting is about to start."

My body feels the immediate loss of warmth as Blair bolts off me and across to her desk, adjusting her dress and running her hands through her hair. She uses her fingers to wipe around her mouth and then stills for a minute, closing her eyes.

Same, I think. I need a moment of silence, too.

It's also obvious I'm going to need more than a moment to collect myself before we walk into the meeting, so I tell Blair to go ahead and I'll catch up. Plus, I'm trying to avoid the regret she looks like she may share with me.

On my way out, Stella tries to avoid eye contact but says a quick hello. She wasn't sitting at her desk when we walked in, so I'm not sure how much she heard. I say hello and try not to make things any more awkward than they already are.

When I make it to the conference room, I see Lance talking to Blair. Her shoulders are pulled up high, and she seems tense. He looks like a total douchebag, leaning against the wall and looking anywhere but directly at her while delivering what I'm guessing is not anything she's happy to hear.

She spins around and stalks to the exit. I start toward her to see what's going on, but she gives me the slightest shake of her head.

"Not right now. Let me go," she says under her breath as she strides by.

I focus on Lance, and he's already moved on, taking his seat at the head of the table.

"Wyatt! How's everything going? Looks like you're making fantastic progress. I had a call with The Manhattan Group, and they were thrilled with everything they've received from us so far. Great work." Lance motions me over to sit next to him.

"It's Blair you should be praising. She's done all the hard work. I'm simply the messenger at this point."

"That's great to hear. We're one big family around here. A win for one is a win for all of us. I'm not into keeping score on any of this, especially during a time when everyone should work for the greater good of our business."

It's clear he's not interested in giving Blair any credit. When he makes a move to start the meeting, I ask, "Should we wait for Blair?"

"She's no longer needed. We have an excellent overview of the agency, but now it's time to talk about where we can make cuts to get the balance sheet where it needs to be. I've talked with our finance teams, and we think it makes sense to start with any overlap or redundant headcount."

I nod, but it makes no sense to exclude her. She would be a great advisor on role clarity and what might be frivolous. I feel Lance does not know what most of the positions at this agency do if they are outside the scope of signing talent. Even then, I'm not sure he's clued in on all the nuance around agent workload.

"So, what's the low-hanging fruit, then?" Lance looks around the table at the crowd of confused eyes glancing back and forth at one another.

"I'm not sure what you mean, sir," a woman across the table says.

"Tell me who would be the easiest to cut. No drama, minimal impact to budget or workload." Lance leans back like this whole meeting is boring to him.

I look around the table and realize nobody knows how to respond. He's literally looking for a list of names that accomplish the goal and doesn't make extra work for him. He has no concern for what processes could be impacted, the potential loss of historical knowledge, or even a gap in skill set that might occur.

"We should probably look at everyone who's on an employment contract first," I say. "It's not a foolproof way to create a list, but it is something we could use to determine where to start. We can look at upcoming contracts that expire between now and the end of the year. Depending on how the language in the contract reads, it may be as simple as just not renewing them."

"Excellent. That's what I'm talking about. Earning your

pay today, Wyatt!" Lance claps his hand on my shoulder and uses it to help him up out of his chair. "It sounds like you've got this figured out, so I'll expect a list by the end of the week."

He walks out of the meeting room, and I look around the table at faces that mirror the disbelief I have.

twenty-four

. . .

BLAIR

"READY TO GO?" Stella says, snapping me out of my daydream. She's standing in front of my desk with a few files in her arms and a Chloe tote bag over her left shoulder.

"What?"

"Roundtable photoshoot. With Sophia. You said you wanted to go, so I made arrangements for us... We don't have to if you've changed your mind?"

Stella looks at me with her head tilted to the side and one eyebrow raised.

"Yes. It slipped my mind for a minute. Of course. Let's go." I push back from my desk and ask her if she has the prompts I want Sophia to review from past roundtables.

"Yes, yes. I've done all of that. What's up with you? You seem really distracted this week."

I'm totally distracted. I can't stop thinking about Wyatt in my office yesterday. After the shame spiral I went down for giving into such a public display of lust, I remembered why I fell for him in the first place. We had an undeniable spark.

Yes, there was a level of physical attraction, but there was more to it. A level of comfort and trust from the first time we met. Even when he started dating Holly, we were close.

I'm seeing everything from a different perspective now. The way he would call me as soon as the class schedules came out to see if ours overlapped. How, every time Holly was away for a dance competition, we'd get together to watch movies or our favorite TV shows. I felt like he belonged to me, and I belonged to him.

But knowing why things changed, why he got back with Holly, that what he felt for me was never the issue, has me all mixed up.

I understand the pressure his parents put on him and how everything can feel out of your control when you are young, but a stubborn part of me is hanging on to my anger at how it happened. He says he wanted to reach out, but it sounds like he moved on just fine. He didn't seem to need any kind of closure at all.

So, now I'm confused because my body and heart want to forgive him. In fact, I can't get my body to listen to any reason when he's around.

But my mind is being a little bitch.

Lance pops his head into my office before we can leave. "Blair, have a minute?"

"Sure, come on in." I signal to Stella to give me just a minute.

I'm still furious he dismissed me from the meetings yesterday, but anytime Lance pops into my office, it puts me on edge. It's a nightmare trying to get any time and attention from him when you need him for something, but he always seems to find time for you if there's a problem. You can tell you're in for some feedback if he starts off with generous compliments. It's a sick trap to put you at ease before he rips you to shreds.

I can tell this isn't a friendly visit as soon as he leans back in the chair across from my desk and puts his right ankle over his knee. The classic agent man spread.

"I'm not interrupting, am I?" he asks.

"We're just on our way to the Actress Roundtable, but I have a few minutes. What's on your mind?"

"Oh, yes, Wyatt mentioned Sophia was taking part in that little article."

The only thing more cringe than his snubbing the press is the obscene number of photos of him with celebrities hanging all over his office walls.

I don't take the bait.

"How come you haven't signed her yet? It's like you don't even care if you work here at all," Lance says, adding in his fake laugh to cover the passive-aggressive comment.

I keep my face composed. It's only been a few weeks, and he knows how much time it can take to court a big name.

"I'm definitely working on it. That's why we're headed over to meet her now."

"Hmm."

"Did you need anything else? We should really get going."

"Actually, I was curious about something. Is Sophia the only person you are talking to right now?"

I take a beat before I answer. I'm not sure where he's headed with this question. He may want to know that I'm dedicating all my time to signing a big name, or he may think I should have several names almost ready to sign right now.

"It's just Sophia, but I'm working on a few new projects for clients already on the roster." I hope that settles any possible unease he may have.

"That's fantastic. Exactly what I wanted to hear."

"Oh."

"Blair, don't sound so surprised. You sign more women than anyone else at this agency and place them with fantastic projects, and you are still one of the highest performers. Some might think you need more testosterone on your roster, but it looks like you are doing just fine without it." He rises off the couch and knocks on my desk twice.

That's a backhanded compliment. I'm highly suspicious.

"Thanks."

"Oh, can you have Stella send over any background info you have on Sophia? I want to make sure I'm fully briefed in case we run into each other here in the office or out in the wild."

And there it is. He doesn't think I can close the deal, so he wants to study up so he can jump in if he thinks it's necessary.

"Of course. I'll get it over to you today."

"Great. What a stroke of luck that you and her brother go way back." He grabs a mint out of the candy jar on my desk and gives me a wink as he pops it into his mouth.

My stomach drops as a wave of heat radiates up my body. What the fuck does that mean?

Stella interrupts with a time check before I can respond, and I shake off the twinge of suspicion that Lance is up to something. I would say he's jealous that I have Sophia and is trying to rattle me, but it seems more calculated than that.

As soon as Lance walks out, I drag Stella to the car while I fill her in on our conversation, letting her know he's peacocking around Sophia but made a weird Wyatt comment.

"Does he know about you two?" she asks.

"If anything was mentioned, it would have been an innocent comment from Wyatt about how we went to school together. Lance is a pig and is trying to make it sound like more."

Even if it was more.

Even if I'm wondering if it could be more now.

"I have a confession to make. I may have, um, kissed Wyatt in my office yesterday." I bite my lip and look over at her to see her reaction. She gives me the side eye.

"No, really? Shocker."

My laugh echoes in the parking garage, and I'm sure she can see my face turning bright red.

"Fine. I didn't think it was that obvious, though!" I try to hide my embarrassment as we buckle up and head out.

"Do you like him?" Stella asks.

"I've always liked him. That's the problem. And now I have this false sense of hope that we could go right back to how we were back then, and I know that's not possible."

"Why not?"

"Because I always do this," I tell her. "I get caught up in the moment of lust and the idea of what could be. But it's never what really is."

"I don't know. It looks like you both like each other. He's obviously obsessed with you."

I think about what she says and wonder if that is true. I thought he felt that strongly about me once before, but the moment he was pressured, he caved and just did the simple thing. How would he react under pressure now? I have no idea what his career ambitions or even personal ambitions are. Does he even want to be in a relationship? Would he blow off anything we might have for his career?

"He was once before, and look how that turned out."

"I don't think you can hold the past against him. You're both completely different people now. And you've both grown from that experience." She grabs my hand and gives it a squeeze. "If you feel a connection to him, you owe it to yourself to explore it."

"I'm not sure it's a connection. More like sexual attraction." I try to laugh at the idea that it's anything more than a little lust, but the look from Stella says she knows it's more than that. From that look alone, I know I'm totally screwed.

"Alright, let's go see some bad-ass women, then," Stella says as we pull up to studio valet. She shifts us from the heavy topic, knowing I'm not ready to go any deeper, and I appreciate it.

I wanted to come today because it's a roundtable interview with seven Oscar-winning women who, in some form, were the first in their category. Sophia is there because she's the most recent winner. I know the questions and topics discussed will be a gold mine of insight. I can't wait to hear from these women firsthand the struggles and obstacles they face in this industry, not just the edited soundbites that make it seem like we're making progress.

I see Sophia laughing with the other women and head that way.

Stella whispers as we walk up. "What did I do in a past life to deserve to be around such gorgeous and powerful women?"

I'm not sure what I did in a past life to deserve her. These women would be lucky to know her. I lean in to hug Sophia and Stella holds her arms out for a hug, too.

"Hey," Sophia says, "I wanted to see if we could talk about arrangements for Jake's wedding before you leave today."

That invite feels so random, yet I'm almost desperate for any excuse to see more of Wyatt. It felt like maybe he felt the same way when he tossed out the invitation to join him.

"I haven't decided if I'm going yet," I say.

"Why not?" Sophia asks.

"Why wouldn't I go to a wedding of someone I've never met with a guy I haven't seen since high school?"

"You've seen him a lot lately," Stella interjects.

"You're going," Sophia says. "I'm not letting you talk your way out of it!"

Her smile suggests she can read every dirty thought I'm having about her brother and knows I won't be able to resist the invite.

She's not wrong.

"What if I promise to hire hair and makeup to help you both get ready for the event?" Stella offers.

I look over at Sophia and see her eyes pleading with me.

"Fine. I'll talk to Wyatt."

twenty-five

. . .

WYATT

THIS IS the first time I've gotten a good look at Blair's house in the daylight. The white stucco and navy shutters and front door give the small bungalow a coastal feel. A covered porch sits on one side, featuring a wall of windowed doors that slide open for easy access to the outdoor living space. Two cozy chairs and a couch complete the look. It's exactly something I would imagine her living in, and I wonder what the inside looks like.

Blair is already waiting outside on the porch steps for me. I check the time again to make sure I'm not late. As I park and exit the car, she walks down to meet me.

"You look stunning," I say.

My eyes roam her body from top to bottom, taking in the light purple dress she's wearing. It's strapless, with a structured bodice showcasing her curves. The flowing skirt hits the ground but slits on both sides of the dress, so when she walks, I see layers of fabric tangled with her bare legs and strappy heels.

"Thank you." She watches me appreciate every curve of her body. "You look nice."

When my hand grazes her upper arm as I help her into the car, I notice the goosebumps, and a thrill runs up my spine, knowing I affect her. "This old thing?"

That gets me a smile.

I'm already dressed in my best-man tux so I can have more time with Blair and be available to help Jake with whatever he may need without worrying about when I can get ready.

I slide into the driver's seat and fasten my seat belt before looking over at her.

"All ready?"

I reach out to squeeze her hand and am relieved when she doesn't pull away.

"Before we go, we should talk about the other day in my office." She hesitates but then turns slightly in her seat to face me.

"Sure. We can talk about anything you want."

"I think I just got caught up in the nostalgia of everything, and I'm sorry. It was unprofessional, and I don't want to lead you on at all." She's twisting the bracelets on her wrist as she talks, avoiding direct eye contact.

I don't respond immediately, giving her space to say more. I regret nothing, and I'm willing to wait if she needs time to work through her confused emotions.

"It's obvious we have an attraction to each other, or had an attraction, but we are completely different people now. You know nothing about me, and I know nothing about you." She finds her confidence and meets my stare.

"You admit there's an attraction?" I say, attempting to lighten the mood a little, but I understand what she is saying. As much as I want to ignore our working relationship, she's not wrong that we should remain professional. At least for now.

I place my hand on her thigh. She looks down at it and then back up at me with heat in her eyes. There's no denying we have a connection. I pull my hand back and focus on the road ahead. "I understand what you are saying, but I'd like to think we could be friends. I enjoy having you back in my life, and I'll take whatever I can get."

As soon as I say it, I hate how it feels. I don't want to be just friends.

When I look over at her, she's smiling, but there's something in her eyes that looks like she might hate that label just as much as I do.

"Friends, then." She shifts back to face forward in her seat and then turns her head toward me again. "So, friend, tell me about this wedding."

I fill her in on Jake and Lauren, how they've been engaged forever and most of us weren't sure if it would ever happen. Lauren surprised all of us, including Jake, with a last-minute decision on a wedding date only two months ago.

When we arrive, I leave the keys with the valet. I can already see my mother through the lobby doors, walking toward us with her arms stretched out, ready to hug me.

"Come here. Oh, I've missed you so much!" She has quite a death grip for such a petite woman. "Stop making excuses and come home for dinner soon."

"Hi, Mom. Missed you, too," I say while wrapping my arms around her.

"Here, I want you to meet Blair. She's Sophia's—"

"Blair! It's so nice to see you again. Sophia shared that you two reconnected!"

Blair doesn't escape the hug from my mom, but the smile lighting up her face tells me she doesn't mind one bit.

My mother leads us through the lobby and toward the wall of windows where the setup for the ceremony is underway on the beach.

"Hi again!" Sophia says as she hugs Blair. They spent the morning together with hair and makeup artists. Seeing both her and my mother embracing Blair gives me a sense of calm. It's like she belongs to me. This is what it would feel like if she were mine.

Before Blair can respond, my father arrives through the back entry, and I stiffen. Blair glances at me and moves in closer, noticing the change in me. I relax a little and appreciate the protective move.

"Wyatt, son! I didn't know you were here already." He reaches out for a handshake and pulls me in for a quick, one-handed tap on the back.

"We just arrived. This is Blair."

"Nice to meet you, Blair."

Blair reaches for his extended hand. "Nice to meet you, too."

"Blair is the agent I've been telling you about," Sophia says.

"She's with TWA?" My father's gaze darts over to me

before returning to her. "I've heard about all the changes happening. Hopefully, it's all going well."

"Wyatt's been a fantastic partner. We wouldn't be in such good shape without him." Blair looks my way, waiting for me to respond, but I don't.

"Is that so?" My father's eyes drift down to her hand resting on my arm, but Sophia interrupts before he can share whatever it is he thinks he sees here.

"You might remember her. She and Wyatt went to high school together."

"I used to work at the country club. It was a long time ago. You probably don't remember me."

"Blair?" He laughs, and I prepare for the impact. "Wyatt, is this the girl that had you so distracted you were going to throw away your entire future?"

Blair's mouth drops open, and the blood rushes through my ears, drowning out all the surrounding sounds.

"I was a distraction?" A look of confusion passes over her face.

"Dad!" Sophia yells at the same time my mom reaches to pull him away from the conversation, but not before we all hear him say, "I thought he was bringing that Bethany woman."

"I better go find Jake," I say, grabbing Blair's hand so she'll follow me to the exit. "We'll catch up with you in a bit."

Sophia nods, a look of understanding crossing her face.

Once we're away from the others, I stop and hang my head. I should have expected this. Taking a deep breath, I turn to face her.

"Who's Bethany?"

"What? Nobody. She's a colleague from New York. Just a family friend."

"I ruined your life."

"No. Absolutely not."

She crosses her arms in front of her. "Right. Just someone who almost convinced you to throw away your entire future."

I place my hands on her arms and bend down a little to meet her eye to eye.

"I need you to hear me when I tell you this. You are the only person who gave a shit about what I wanted. You were not a distraction. You were a savior. You made me believe in myself. Every time you walked into a room, my heart skipped a beat, and I couldn't breathe. Everything about you is beautiful. Your smile, your laugh. You make everything in my life brighter. I'm drawn to you in ways I can't fully explain. Even now, after all these years, that feeling hasn't faded."

Blair doesn't respond, and for a minute, I fear she's going to walk away. After holding my eyes for another beat, she nods.

"Ok."

***

My best friend is officially getting married. I'm excited for Jake, and he's certainly spared no expense. I see Blair seated on the groom's side in the second row. She looks beautiful, and it makes me think about the day this will be us celebrating. I want it all with her. She catches me staring and I hope that look means she's having the same thoughts. We belong together.

The start time was delayed a bit, so now Jake and Lauren are rushing through the vows so the fireworks will still sync up with "I now pronounce you..." I want to roll my eyes, but something about seeing my best friend overwhelmed with happiness has me sentimental.

After the ceremony, I find Blair at the front family and friends' table. I sit down and grab her hands in mine.

"Everything ok?"

"Yeah. Had a little scare before the ceremony and some drama during pictures, but all's well now." I lean over to kiss her and I can't keep my hands off her legs, running them over her skin and dress. "And I missed you."

She smiles but it feels like she's holding back. Before I can question it she laces her fingers between mine.

"Is that why the ceremony started late?"

"Yeah. She refused to walk down the aisle until Jake had her grandfather's handkerchief in his lapel pocket. He forgot to bring it, so Jake's cousin had to run to his house."

"You're kidding."

"I wish I was."

"It must be really sentimental. Wow." She turns toward to front of the room to look at the happy couple. "What happened during photos?"

"That was more about Lauren dictating where everyone would stand. She did a ton of solo pics and got upset when she overheard someone ask why she didn't do this before the ceremony."

"I agree—why didn't she?"

"This is typical Lauren. Jake loves her and he's oblivious. I used to get irritated by it, but if he's happy, then I'm happy."

"You're a good man, Wyatt Bradford. Some might even say the best man."

I lean in to kiss her again and glance around the table to make sure she won't be lonely while I attend to my best man responsibilities. I'm on deck for the speech, after it's cake, and then I'm free to enjoy the rest of the evening with Blair. I plan to wrap my arms around her on the dance floor and prove to her she is the best thing that ever happened to me.

twenty-six

. . .

BLAIR

I'M SPIRALING.

Sophia's been swept away by Jake's cousin and he's currently spinning her on the dance floor, while I'm sitting alone at the friends and family table. With Wyatt's family. His father is deeply distracted by his phone, while his mother is catching up with Jake's mom. I keep hearing his father's words in my head. *I thought he was coming with Bethany?* It feels like déjà vu.

I'm so confused because Wyatt is saying all of the right things, but I feel like we've been here before. Wanting to be together is not our problem, but expectations from his family —his father—seem to still haunt him. I don't trust that our feelings will ever outweigh his obligation.

As the end of the evening nears, and the groomsmen head out to the dance floor to celebrate Jake, I slip away quietly, careful not to draw attention to myself. I need some time to think. I know Wyatt will be upset that I left without him, but

I'm not in the right headspace to talk through anything yet. I don't even know what I want. My heart pounds in my chest as I make my way through the crowd, and my mind races with everything Wyatt's dad said. Distraction. Almost ruined his life. The words play on repeat in my head like a cruel mantra.

And Bethany—another perfect match Wyatt's dad lined up for him. Why did I let my feelings get the best of me again? Why didn't I learn my lesson the first time?

I'm exhausted when I get home. Emotionally, I'm wiped, but I find myself pulled to my closet to dig out the old memory box I haven't touched in years. It's a shrine to Wyatt, filled with pieces of our past—pictures, movie stubs, little notes we passed in class. I grab the box and a bottle of wine and spread out on the couch, too tired to change right now.

As I sift through our past, I can't help but feel the familiar tug in my chest. How did everything go so wrong? I stare at a photo of us on the back of a golf cart. His arm is wrapped around my waist like he never wants to let go. My hand rests on his thigh, a casual touch that feels anything but casual when I think about it now. My head is turned in his direction, mid-laugh, my eyes crinkling at the corners. I can't remember what was so funny, but the way he's looking at me—like I'm the only person in the world—makes my heart skip a beat even now. It's impossible to reconcile that boy with the one who hurt me or the man who could destroy me all over again.

I hear a knock at my door and try to ignore it until I hear Wyatt's voice calling my name. When I finally open the door, he looks relieved.

"Can I come in?"

I want to tell him to go away and slam the door in his face, but I've spent the last hour revisiting our past and all the good times we had, so I let him in.

He's quiet as he looks at the mess of memories spread all over the couch. Then he walks over for a closer look. "What's all this?"

"Us."

"You kept all this?"

When I finally glance up, he looks...relieved. Hopeful, even. As he steps closer to me, I can see the determination in his eyes.

"Blair, I'm sorry about earlier."

"I guess your father isn't a fan of mine."

He takes my hands in his. "What my father thinks doesn't matter. What I think does. And I choose you. I'm sorry for everything—for the past, for tonight—but you have to believe me when I say that what we have is real. It's always been real."

His words hit me hard, and I want so badly to believe him. But a part of me is still scared, waiting for the other shoe to drop.

"How do I know this isn't just going to end the same way it did before?" I ask, my voice barely above a whisper.

He squeezes my hands gently, and his gaze is steady and sincere. "Because I've learned from my mistakes. And because I'm not letting you go again. Not this time."

I search his eyes, looking for any sign of doubt, but all I see is truth and a vulnerability I've never seen in him before.

Maybe, just maybe, this time can be different. And maybe, just maybe, I can let myself believe that, too.

"Blair, I don't want to be friends."

I nod because I'm not sure any sound would come out if I were to try to speak. My heart is racing, and I know I should insist he go home.

But I don't want to.

Wyatt brushes my lips with his, barely touching them, and slides his tongue over my lips and into my mouth. Our tongues twirl as his hands find my waist and gently pull me closer to him. He runs them over my hips and finds the slit in my skirt, giving him access to my upper thigh. Then his thumb grazes the inside of my thigh, gently teasing the possibilities.

"We're not friends," I say, more as a fact than a question.

"No."

I push into his lips more urgently, and he pulls me over to the couch, where he sits and positions me on top of him so I'm straddling his legs. The only thing between us is the strip of lace I have on and the thin fabric of his slacks. I can feel how much he wants me.

As I unbutton his shirt, his lips and tongue caress my neck and shoulder. His body is intoxicating. He's athletic and masculine, with hard edges and ridges outlining his abs. I flatten my hand against his stomach and take my time, rubbing up his chest to peel off his shirt.

"Your body is incredible." I've missed it.

He digs his hands into my backside, giving my ass a squeeze before he runs them up my back, finds the top of my zipper, and slowly drags it down. His breath catches, and his eyes gleam with desire when he sees I'm not wearing a bra.

"So is yours."

His hands drop to my thighs, and his fingers tickle me as he glides them closer to my center. He presses his lips against my collarbone, dragging his tongue across my chest just above my breasts. Then he kisses me right over my heart. It's something he started doing when we became more than friends.

It's an intimate gesture. A message that he owns it.

It gives me the courage to let go and trust him.

I move my hands down to the top of his pants, resting my fingers inside the front waistband. As soon as I do, he lifts me off the couch.

"Bedroom," he commands.

"Down the hall, last door on the right."

My legs wrap around his waist as he carries me to my bed, and then I'm on my back while he settles in between my legs, spreading them wide.

I stop breathing for a minute as warmth floods me.

"Blair, if you don't want this, please tell me now."

Wyatt holds eye contact with me as he gently pulls the delicate fabric of my dress over my hips, down my legs and lets it fall to the floor. Then he sits back on his knees, eyes roaming over my body as he waits for me to respond.

"You are so beautiful," he tells me.

I want this. I've wanted this for years. I hesitate because there's no turning back. Once we cross this line, I won't be able to be just friends. He dips his head down to kiss my upper thigh and then moves up slowly. I feel his tongue lick up the seam of my panties.

"Wyatt," I whisper.

"I love hearing my name on your lips. It's the only thing I want to hear from you as you shatter around me."

He crawls up my body to put his mouth on mine, and a soft moan escapes my lips. Then his hand dips into my panties, and his fingers slide down and slip inside me. He was always so good with his hands. I respond by pressing my hips up, asking for more.

I can feel Wyatt's smile on my lips and then he kisses down my body again. He grabs the sides of my panties and pulls them down over my thighs and off my legs.

"Open wide for me. Let me see that beautiful pussy."

He's sliding his tongue from the bottom to the top of my slit before I can even open my legs all the way, and the warm, soft sensation has me buzzing with pleasure.

I put my hands on his head as he uses his tongue to circle my clit, and then I feel him insert two fingers inside. Already, I feel like I'm going to explode.

I feel a rush of emotions: excitement, fear, and a flicker of hope. The chemistry between us is undeniable. My body responds instinctually, remembering exactly how right it feels to be with him. I've been afraid to open myself up to him again, but could we truly make it work this time? The thought of a future without him terrifies me, and I'm worried I'm in too deep already.

"I'm close."

"I know, baby. Let go for me."

His tongue circles and flicks my clit again, and my body grips his fingers. I see stars when I slam my eyes shut. My body shudders, and he gently pulls his mouth away but places his thumb to rub against me, stretching out my orgasm.

"Wyatt," I say like a prayer.

"I know," He says as he crawls back up my body. His lips are still shiny from tasting me.

"Let me…" I start to rise, but he places his large hand across my stomach to hold me in place and push me back down.

"Next time. I need to be inside you now."

I push his pants down to his thighs, and he takes over from there, taking them all the way off, leaving him in his boxer briefs. He leans down to kiss me again, and his tongue searches for mine. He breaks the kiss to run his lips down my neck and between my breasts, twirling his tongue around my nipples, sending a twinge down my body.

I reach down to push his underwear off, and his massive cock springs out, leaning against my thigh. It's heavy, hard, and huge. I know we've been here before, but he looks so much bigger.

"Like what you see?" Wyatt smirks at me as he reaches out to grab a condom from his wallet.

"It's bigger than I remember."

"You can handle it. We'll go slow. You set the pace."

He rolls on the condom and slides back between my legs, using his arms to hover above me. After reaching up to push my hair away from my forehead, he stills for a minute.

"God, you don't know how many times I've thought of this, dreamed of this."

He drops his forehead to mine, and I close my eyes. I've been dreaming of him since we were sixteen years old. I pull him down on top of me and tilt my hips to feel him against me.

He adjusts to put his tip at my entrance and whispers, "Are you sure?"

I nod.

"I need to hear you say it. Tell me you want this."

"I want you, Wyatt. Please."

I gasp as he pushes in. He waits and teases my lips with his tongue. He's so big, stretching me almost to the point of pain. Then he inches in a little more, giving me time to adjust before he finally thrusts in one last time, putting him deep inside me. He waits there a minute, breathing hard.

"I'm ok. You can move."

"I need a minute, or this is going to be over before it starts." He covers my lips, and I can feel his smile.

Slowly, he moves in and out of me, finding a rhythm that makes my insides tingle. Already, I can feel the buildup happening again.

"I can feel you tightening around me. It's driving me crazy, Blair. You're going to make me come too fast."

"It feels so good. I need more."

He pulls my knee to his hip and quickens his pace, pushing into me harder. He's touching parts inside of me that I thought were a myth. Our bodies find a punishing rhythm, creating a sheen of sweat between us. He reaches down to put his thumb on my clit, and immediately, I'm coming as I whisper his name over and over.

His pace gets erratic, and his release comes right after mine. He leans his forehead on mine and drops tiny kisses across my nose and cheeks. His body is still heavy on top of mine.

"I don't think I can keep things professional anymore, Blair," Wyatt says as his lips find my heart.

I look up at him, and his eyes are serious, his brows pulled together.

I run my fingers across his jaw and rest my hand on his chest.

"Me, either."

twenty-seven

. . .

WYATT

I'M BACK in the TWA offices this afternoon, disappointed that I missed seeing Blair. It's been three days since the wedding and moving out of the friend zone. We've been texting but tiptoeing around the s-e-x topic. But at least we're talking. My mind is operating in 4K definition, replaying the moments with Blair at her house: my hands sliding over her curves, the softness of her pressing into me, how sinking into her felt like home. Just thinking about it puts pressure on my zipper all over again.

I hate how my father almost scared her off, but it's almost like it made something click within her, too. It brought the clarity she needed to get past what happened between us, but I know she still has some doubts. I need time with her.

Lance is next to the coffee dispensers, talking to his head of legal. He spots me, gives a wave, and, in his booming voice, announces my arrival. "There's the guy making sure we make everything happen!"

I give him a courtesy nod and a tight-lipped smile as I

grab a seat at the conference table. When he sits down next to me, I groan internally.

"I actually wanted to talk to you about a confidential matter," Lance whispers as he leans toward me.

"Sure, what is it?"

My nerves kick in for a minute as the guilt of crossing the professional line with Blair creeps into the back of my head.

"Hypothetically, if one of our executives was having a consensual but casual relationship with a colleague and that colleague was on the list of employees to be terminated, could that employee sue us?"

"That depends," I say carefully.

"On what?"

"Well, is the employee a subordinate of the executive? Are there any policies in place that prohibit workplace relations? Is the employee on the impacted list for a legitimate reason?"

Lance slaps his hand on my shoulder and gives me that grin-fucker smile: all teeth, squinty eyes, and absolutely zero humanity behind it.

"She's not a direct subordinate. Anyone can date, but it's at their own risk. So, if shit goes south, not my fault. I don't want any of that drama falling on TWA. As for the list, I'm sure anyone on it is legitimate. I wouldn't want to jeopardize our agency and risk any legal action."

"Lots of things can go south even if there's not a dating policy. I've seen many consensual, casual relationships turn into serious harassment cases."

He's not even listening to me. Instead, his eyes are

roaming around the room, searching for the next conversation to jump into.

"Of course, Wyatt. I understand. And thanks for keeping this just between us. You've been such a great asset through all of this. I'll make sure your father knows how much we appreciate all your help."

I'm one hundred percent sure he never speaks with my father. And when he turns to talk to the head of HR, I know our conversation is over.

While we wait for the others to arrive, I check my phone and scroll back through the messages from Blair. She's been sending me a few of the photos she kept of us. It's a safe way for her to lean into the idea of us, and I want her to remember how great we were together.

ME

I didn't know agents took vacation days.

BLAIR

Just because I'm not in the office it doesn't mean I'm not working 😉

ME

I actually believe you. You're relentless.

BLAIR

Is that a compliment?

ME

It's admiration.

BLAIR

Hmm. What am I missing at TWA?

ME

Merger meetings. And your boss blinding everyone when the reflection from his super white teeth glistens every time he smiles.

BLAIR

😂😂😂

ME

Plans this weekend?

The dots pop up and disappear, and this repeats a few times. I realize I'm holding my breath. I shouldn't have given her an opportunity to make up plans before I could ask her to go on a date with me.

BLAIR

Nope.

The breath that leaves my chest catches the attention of the lady sitting next to me, and I get a worried frown from her.

"It's good news," I tell her as I lift my phone quickly. To avoid any conversation, I start typing.

ME

Can I take you out to dinner?

BLAIR

Call me later and we can talk about it?

It's not a no. And we haven't spoken on the phone yet. I'm taking this as a win.

ME

Absolutely. Don't work too hard today.

BLAIR

(photo of her legs on a raft in a pool with a fruity drink in her hand)

I can't help the grin that creeps across my face.

"It must be fantastic news, with that smile," the woman next to me says as she passes over a packet of stapled documents.

I tuck my phone away and look through the papers in front of me. It's the list of employees to be fired, along with the cost reductions for TWA.

Lance starts the meeting by reminding everyone that this information is confidential, and I get a chill when he turns his gaze on me. There's a bit of determined arrogance behind his eyes.

"Some of you will see familiar names on the list," he says. "I realize keeping professional and personal relationships separate can be hard, but I expect everyone in this room to adhere to the NDA. If any names are leaked from this list, there will be an investigation and consequences."

My blood runs cold when I see Blair's name at the top of the list.

"Some of the names on this list bring in the most revenue. Does the decision to lay them off make sense?" I say.

"We're merging with the largest sports agency in North America. High-earners are a dime a dozen," Lance responds.

I realize I'm biting my tongue when I taste the tang of copper. My eyes must reveal the distain I'm feeling right now.

"I hope this isn't too personal for you. I know you and Blair just reconnected," Lance says quietly as he leans into me when the CFO takes over the meeting to discuss the financial impact.

"Of course not," I say.

I don't appreciate the assumption from Lance that anything personal is going on between Blair and me. Even if there is. I'm not sure how he would even know. This guy is a first-class douche. It's all a fucking game to him. And I know how to play it, too.

twenty-eight

. . .

I LOOK at my face in the mirror, surprised I don't see any dark circles. In fact, I look good, rested, with a fresh flush on my face. It's probably because I've slept so well. I guess multiple orgasms will do that to a girl. Plus, when I sleep, I can pretend that everything is perfect with Wyatt.

My logical brain knows this is a bad idea, but my body does not care. I felt that spark ignite again, like no time had passed. I thought I had made it up in my head, a feeling amplified by heartbreak. It's stronger now. Years of regret and longing are edging us this time. It's exhilarating and terrifying at the same time.

I pull my hair into a ponytail, grab my AirPods, and walk out the door. I need to process all this, and only two things help me think: running and Jess.

ME

I'm going for a run.

JESS

I'll get the wine ready.

I don't know what I would do without her. She has always known exactly what I need, even before I do.

I'm covered in a sheen of sweat when I arrive at Jess's place, and she opens the door with a wet hand towel and a glass of chardonnay.

"I'm assuming this is about Wyatt?" she says as she turns back to the kitchen.

"I slept with him."

I've never seen Jess whip around so quickly, and the look on her face makes me laugh so hard I collapse.

"Way to jump right in there. Say more."

I recap what his father said about me distracting him to the point of ruin and how he mentioned he expected a different plus-one for Wyatt. Then I fast-forward to the part where I left the reception early, but how he showed up on my doorstep after, and then we were naked minutes later.

She sets a bowl of popcorn and a plate of twizzlers next to our glasses of wine. "Please, be specific. Size, creativity, language..." Jess begs me.

I ignore her and confess how comfortable I felt with him. It was obviously different this time, but also not. It felt familiar. Right. I'm desperate to give in to the emotions, but I'm cautious about getting too attached. I can't help the feeling that I've been here before. My mind replaying my track record with men.

"I see your brain trying to figure out how to shut this down."

"Yep. I have to shut it down, right?"

"Why?" Jess is sipping on her wine and giving me that quizzical look over the rim of her glass. I stepped right into her web, and now we're going to have to play the "so what, what if" game.

"Jess, you know why. Don't do your head tricks on this one."

"Did you like it?"

I lean my head back and rub my hands over my face.

"I'll take that as a yes. Did he like it?"

"I don't know. We haven't talked about it."

Jess is quiet for a minute, knowing I'll say more.

"We're obviously still attracted to each other, and it felt..." I trail off, trying to find the words to explain it. It felt like forever.

"You know what I'm going to say. If it's supposed to happen, it will. No matter how you try to fight it or avoid it. So, just let it be."

Jess has always believed we're all on a path and, when we resist or question things, we're just delaying our destiny. The idea of that sounds great. Permission to just live and enjoy life? Easier said than done.

"I'm not just going to throw myself at him," I say.

"I didn't say that. But if you fall into bed again, so be it."

I lie back and stretch my body across the carpeted living room floor.

"Maybe."

I'm afraid if we spend more time together, I'll believe I could have a happily ever after. And I don't know if I do.

"Ok, I'm calling reinforcements," Jess says and gets up off the floor to grab her phone.

"No! Nobody else can know about this!"

"Calm down. You are too much in your head. I'm just calling Stella over. We can day drink and hang by the pool. You need distractions!"

Jess types on her phone as she walks down the hall. "Stella's on her way." She shouts from her room. "And she's bringing Brandon and Natalie!"

"Who's Natalie?"

"Stella's yoga teacher friend. She's awesome!"

I peel myself off the ground and head to Jess's room to borrow a bathing suit. I'm too distracted to work right now anyway.

"So, don't hold out on us. How was the wedding?" Brandon is already in the pool, his arms hanging over the edge. "Did you meet the parents? Did you go home with Wyatt?"

I almost choke on my drink.

"It was completely normal," I say. "The parents are fine. And no, I didn't go home with Wyatt." Technically, that is true. Hopefully, that's enough detail.

"Come on, spill. You're telling me there was no drama, no mystery, no suspense?"

I laugh. It's clear that spending so much time with actors and actresses has influenced Brandon's appetite for gossip.

"Oh, I don't know. There was probably a little mystery,"

Jessica whispers under her breath. Thankfully, Brandon doesn't hear her.

"I'm sure you have better stories to tell about your Fourth," I say, trying to change the subject.

Stella immediately blushes, and she and Natalie look at each other and then over at Brandon.

"Stella has a new neighbor that she thinks is hunky," Brandon teases.

Jess and I look at Stella, our eyebrows raised.

"I'm so mortified. Right in the middle of getting ready to go out for the night, someone knocked on the door, and when I opened it, there was this God of a man. Think Harry Styles—"

"I'm not sure he was quite up to that level," Brandon says.

"He was so hot I literally lost my words, and when he asked if this was Sam and Delilah's place, I responded with 'Hunky.'" She slaps her hands over her face, and we all burst out laughing.

"I'm sure it wasn't that bad," I reassure her.

"It was that bad," Natalie confirms.

Stella tells us that Sam and Delilah are her neighbors and the Harry lookalike is their nephew. He's just moved to town and is staying with his aunt and uncle until he can find his own place.

The three of them are gossiping about how Stella will never be able to face him and how nervous she is about running into him again when my phone buzzes.

I'm not even aware of the huge grin stretched across my lips when I see Wyatt's name. We exchange a few texts, and when I look up, Jess is staring.

"What?" I ask.

"You tell me."

"He wants to take me to dinner."

"I'm guessing from the glow on your face that you're going."

Hell, yes, I am.

twenty-nine

. . .

WYATT

I RAISE my hand to knock on Blair's door, but she opens it before I can. I suck in a breath. My eyes take her in, starting with what she is wearing: a short black silk dress, hitting mid-thigh, with thin straps and a scooped neckline. It teases me and immediately makes all the blood in my body rush to my dick. When my eyes make it back up to her face, her eyebrows are raised as if to say, *Like what you see?*

"You look gorgeous."

"Thank you. So do you." She bites her bottom lip like she's nervous. "Shall we go?"

I walk her to the car, open the door, and help her in. When she lowers to get into the seat, her dress rises, coming dangerously close to showing me what might be under it. I shut the door and do my best to adjust the discomfort in my pants before I get into the car.

I'm taking her to a nice place in Santa Monica. I'd be lying if I didn't admit I also chose this restaurant because of its proximity to my house. If everything goes well, I'm hoping I can convince her to come home with me.

While I've dated a few women, I never thought a relationship would be in the cards for me. Most women want more than I can offer, or they like my bank account or proximity to fame. But Blair doesn't care about all that.

For the first time, I let myself think about a future with her, and when I look over at her, she looks like mine.

At the restaurant, I take Blair's hand in mine as the hostess leads us to the back.

"This is awfully romantic." She looks up at me before she slides into the booth, and I move in right next to her.

"I'm shooting my shot. I hope that's obvious after what's happened between us."

"We gave into a moment," she says casually. "It doesn't have to mean anything."

I keep my eyes straight ahead as I take a minute to process what she just said. I don't think I misread how she felt. Every touch, every kiss healed the wounds of our past.

"Maybe." I clear my throat, trying to find the courage to say it meant everything.

"Maybe what?"

"It kinda meant something." I chance a glance at her. She's looking at me, waiting to hear more, so I go for it.

"It meant something to me. If it didn't to you, I'll understand. Or I'll try to. But I don't want that to be just a moment. I want more moments with you."

"I think—"

"We can avoid talking about it for now and just enjoy the night," I say, interrupting her to stop her from overthinking this and shutting down any chance we have before we even get started, especially if all she needs is time to adjust to the idea of us together. "We're friends who have reconnected and are attracted to each other. And we both need to eat."

She hesitates but, thankfully, changes the topic. "So, how were the TWA offices yesterday? Did you find the six million in savings everyone is talking about?"

A server arrives to get our drink order just in time. If Blair knew her name was on that cost-savings list, I'm not sure she would be here with me right now, especially since it was my idea that generated the first draft of employees who would be impacted. It never occurred to me that her contract would expire so soon.

"What do you think about all this change happening at TWA?" I ask her, trying to change the subject a little.

"I'm hopeful it's good. The industry is changing, which means the way we all do business has to change. The Manhattan Group has a fantastic women's sports portfolio. That's promising."

"Would you ever consider shifting your focus to represent athletes?"

"No. I mean, never say never, but I don't even really want to stay at TWA forever."

"Really?"

"Don't look so surprised. You know how I like to champion women."

"I do. You say that like you don't do that every day, though."

"It's getting harder."

"So, if not TWA, what would you do?"

"The dream is to open up my own shop, one where the only focus is women and other underrepresented groups."

"An advocate for the snubbed and disregarded."

"Well said." She raises her glass to toast mine, and I relax a little. Maybe getting laid off might not be such bad news to her after all. Maybe it's just the push she needs.

We spend the rest of dinner catching each other up on what our lives are like now. I share more about Jake, what it's like working with my dad, and how watching Sophia blossom into a star has been so surreal. She tells me more about Jess, and I can tell that Jess probably knows more about me than I realize. I find myself laughing more than I have in a long time, and I don't want this night to end.

"Let's take a walk outside."

I lead her out to the back of the restaurant, where a deck stretches out over the beach. On the right, casual lounge seating crowds the fire pits, which radiate heat to chase the chill away. We walk to the left for a little privacy and to take in the ocean's view under the full moon.

Blair props her elbows on the rails, and I stand next to her, close enough to feel the heat of her body, but I keep my hands in my pocket so I'm not tempted to rip that dress off of her.

"It's a beautiful night," she says.

I keep my eyes on her. "It sure is."

She turns and looks up at me, and I pull one hand out of my pocket and place it on the railing, slightly caging her in.

"Thank you for dinner. This was fun."

Being this close to her is intoxicating, and I lean down to kiss her.

She welcomes my lips, and the kiss starts soft and sweet. My lips brush gently across hers with the message that I can be patient and this is real.

She turns toward me, and my hand goes to her hip, squeezing and pulling her close to me. I lean back and look at her to make sure she's ok, and she brings her hands to my chest and tilts her head down.

I put my other hand behind her neck to tilt her head back up to me and meet her lips again, this time with more pressure, pushing my tongue between her lips.

She reciprocates and presses her body even closer, bringing her arms up, wrapping them around my neck, and grazing her fingers through the hair at the back of my head.

We kiss like we're starving, and my hands move from her hips down to palm her ass. When I run my hand down her thigh to lift it, it breaks the spell.

"We should stop. Anyone could walk up at any minute."

"Come home with me."

I return my hands to her waist and pull back so that we are still close but not mashed together. I continue to pepper kisses on her lips, hoping I never have to stop.

"Ok."

I go in for one more deep kiss and then gently cradle her face and neck as I brush her hair aside.

"Let's go." With a smile, I place my hand on the small of her back and guide her out to the valet.

At the front of the restaurant, I hear the woman's voice before I see her.

"Wyatt! Oh, my God! What are you doing here?"

Bethany, my old friend with benefits, walks in and immediately makes a beeline for me with her arms out and a smile on her face. I've avoided seeing her the last few times she's been in town. We've never been exclusive, but I don't want Blair to get the wrong impression.

Blair stiffens and steps away, and I instantly feel the loss.

Bethany wraps her arms around me, and her lips graze the side of my mouth before I can fully pull away. I'm fuming at her rudeness and lack of tact. She can obviously see I'm with Blair.

"Bethany, this is Blair. My date."

She looks Blair up and down with a fake smile plastered on. "Hi, Blair. Nice to meet you."

I glance over and watch as Blair's face pales and she offers a stiff nod in response.

Bethany turns back to me. "Is this why you didn't have time for me this weekend?"

Fuck. This is getting worse by the second. Bethany knows our arrangement was casual. I've got to end this. Just then Blair steps up and loops her arm through mine.

"We better get going, babe." A sense of pride simmers as I realize she's staking her claim.

"Good to see you again, Bethany." I step around her, hoping we can get out of here before this overshadows our night.

I grab Blair's hand, but when we make it to the valet, she pulls it from mine.

"She's the girl from Firefly."

I have no idea what she's talking about. What girl from Firefly? She must see the confusion on my face.

"When you asked me to meet you for dinner. That first time. She was sitting with you at your table when I arrived."

That was the week I blew Bethany off, not knowing I would see Blair again. It was a fluke that we ran into each other that night.

"Is that why you slipped out without saying goodbye?" I ask.

She nods.

"She was there with her colleagues. We weren't together. She just stopped by to say hi."

"And she was supposed to be your plus-one at Jake's wedding."

"I never asked her to go with me to Jake's wedding. That was all my father. He suggested it, and I just ignored him, so he made assumptions."

"You should stay. I can call an Uber. No reason you shouldn't catch up with an old friend. Besides, it's late. I should get home."

Blair is backing up and trying to walk away; I can tell she is rattled. Stepping toward her—I have no intention of letting her escape—I place my hand on her hips and bring her close.

"I'm sorry. Would you believe me if I say it all sounds and looks way worse than it is?"

Her eyes narrow, and her head tilts as if she's saying it's exactly what it looks like.

"Truth?" I say, throwing out our favorite peace treaty.

"Always the truth," she replies.

"Bethany is someone I was seeing casually before I saw you at the studio lot with Sophia. She's from New York, but her firm has an office here in LA, so she travels back and forth. It was a convenient setup for both of us, but it's over."

Blair doesn't say anything, and I can see her mind spinning as doubt about being with me creeps across her face. I realize that it's going to take more than a drive to my house for her to recover from that interaction. It's like a spotlight has just landed on how much we still don't know about each other, on how much time has passed.

Fuck.

"Come on. I'll take you home."

She's quiet on the drive to her house. I walk her to her door, but before she goes in, I pull her back to me. When I tip her chin up, a small sigh passes through her lips.

"I'm sorry. I have a past. But so do you," I tell her. "But there's been no one serious and nobody in quite some time."

She nods but doesn't look away.

"This is moving a little too fast for me," she confesses. "I like you—you know I do—but I need a minute."

I tangle my fingers through hers, not wanting to let go. Then I lean down and kiss her gently.

"Ok. I'll follow your lead."

thirty

. . .

BLAIR

"WHAT HAPPENED? START AT THE BEGINNING."

I fill Jess in on dinner, how we kissed outside by the ocean, and how the evening was easy, fun, and romantic. When I get to the part where I agreed to go home with him, I have to pull the phone back from my ear as she squeals with excitement. Then I have to talk her off the excitement ledge by telling her I didn't end up at his house.

"He said he hasn't been with her since the first time he saw me. But it didn't feel like he's officially shut it down with her."

"Did you ask him?"

"Not exactly. When she walked up, I froze." It was a mix of rage and despair. It totally fucked with my head, and all my insecurities showed up. About how Wyatt chose Holly, Billy chose Kandi, every guy in college didn't choose me... "It just shut down any hope I was feeling."

"How did he react?"

"He pulled back like he'd been burned." I think about what he said, how we both have a past. I just don't know if she is part of his present. "He did introduce me as his date. She was snarky, asking if I was why he couldn't meet her this weekend."

"Bitch!" Jess shouts.

"He got us out of there quickly and took me home."

"You need to talk to him about this. If you like him, tell him."

I sit back in my chair. I came into work so I wouldn't sit around the house and obsess about Wyatt. As I look around my corner office, I feel lucky. It's glamorous, and I'm proud of what I've accomplished here—and the 180-degree views of Hollywood and Beverly Hills aren't terrible, either. Yet, there are days when I would gladly give it all up to run my own agency. Talking about it with Wyatt rekindled something in me.

"Honestly, Jess, it's for the best. I need to focus on work. Lance has all but threatened to throw me under the bus if I don't sign Sophia."

"Asshole."

Tell me about it. Normally, I'm relentless in pursuing new talent. But I know spending more time with Wyatt and Sophia has changed how I'm approaching everything. I don't feel a sense of urgency because I want her to find her perfect match. I think that is me, but I need to know she believes that, too, regardless of how well we get along or if I have history with her brother.

"You heard TWA is laying off like three percent of staff in prep for this merger," Jess says, interrupting my wandering mind.

"I mean, I heard that there were some financial things that needed to be cleaned up. I was part of the early meetings, but it sounded like it was more around systems and processes. I didn't think we would impact actual people. At least not yet."

"Word is there's a list. Apparently, everyone working on the merger is now under an NDA, so I couldn't get a lot of details, but it doesn't sound great."

"Another reason I should stay away from Wyatt. He's deeply embedded in all that work, and I'm sure that would piss Lance off. I just need to focus on signing talent, selling projects, and staying alert around here."

I knew something didn't feel right when Lance asked me to attend the meetings early on and then abruptly shut me out. I can't believe I didn't question it more.

"Ok, but I'm just going to say one thing. You are the total package: gorgeous, smart, talented, funny, kind, and generous. Don't get into your head about if the relationship will work. Protect your heart, but don't close it off."

I hear what she's saying, and logically, I know it's all true, but it's hard to trust my judgment when it comes to relationships. My heart was open with Wyatt and even Billy, but it still fell apart.

"Thanks, Jess, but I don't have the best track record."

"Blair, I love you, but you drive me crazy with this perfection thing. There is no perfect fairy tale."

"Annie and Sam."

"That doesn't count. They're the only couple in the world we know who met as teenagers, married, and still like each other."

"Nathan and Haley."

"Who? I don't know them."

"Daphne and Simon."

"I... Who?"

"Luke and Lorelai."

"Wait, are you just listing TV couples now?"

"Cory and Topanga. Joey and Pacey. Seth and Summer—"

"Stop. I think I've figured out your problem. I don't know

why I didn't figure it out earlier. All this Hollywood story-telling has your brain warped."

"These stories come from somewhere!" I shout.

I know I sound like a crazy, delusional woman. I also know that a Hollywood rom-com isn't real life, but sometimes, I wish it could be.

Jess sighs, and I can tell she's hit her limit with me. She's the best friend anyone could have, but she also shuts shit down when it goes off the rails and she's made her point. Now I'm just annoying her and wasting her time.

"I love you, sweetie. You don't have to decide anything today, but maybe don't shut the door on anything just yet, either. I gotta run, but drinks later?"

"Yeah, I'll text you later. Love you."

"Love you, babe."

I hang up and replay the night in my head. When I think back to our conversation and that kiss, I can't help the smile that creeps onto my face. It's the blonde woman putting her lips on him that sends me into a rage.

I shake the memory from my head and wake up my computer to work. Then I see an email from Wyatt.

TO: Blair Bennett
FROM: Wyatt Bradford
Subj: Second chance?

Hi,

Was hoping I could get a do-over of the ending of our date last night. Can I take you to the Dodgers game tonight?
Please say yes,
Wyatt

I lean back and put my hands over my face because I'm terrified of what this could do to my heart, but I want to see him again. The idea of holding hands with him as we walk through the stadium sets off butterflies in my stomach. I hate how my mind is fighting my heart for the rights to my feelings.

TO: Wyatt Bradford
FROM: Blair Bennett
Subj: RE: Second chance?

I'm only saying yes to the baseball game. All the rest is TBD.
Pick me up at my house.
Cautiously,
Blair

His reply is immediate.

TO: Blair Bennett

FROM: Wyatt Bradford
Subj: RE: RE: Second chance?

I'll take what I can get. All I need is time for the rest.
Hopefully yours,
Wyatt

I lean back in my chair and zone out, thinking about what I might wear tonight. I can see the wall of TVs from the other windows in my office. It has a clear view of Lance's office. Movement catches my eye as he walks through his door, and I jump up with every intention of confronting him about layoffs.

As I race across the open space between our offices, I force myself to take a deep breath and calm down a bit. I need to stay professional. Lance isn't a guy who likes to be challenged, and I've seen him ruin people for less while shining his smile of perfectly white veneers.

"Hey, Blair," he says when I enter his office. "What has you in on the weekend?"

"Hey, Lance. Just catching up on a few things for next week."

"I hope this means you've signed Sophia."

"Close."

"That's what I like to hear."

"How are the merger meetings going?" I grab a mint off his coffee table in an effort to seem uninvested in his answer.

"Everything is going as planned," he says. "You should get on out of here and try to enjoy what's left of your weekend." His dismissal is obvious and direct. He couldn't even look me in the eye as he sidestepped my question, which tells me nothing is going as originally planned.

thirty-one

. . .

WYATT

"YOU ARE ALIVE!" Sophia pulls me inside her house, and I wrap my arms around her, squeezing her tight and kissing her on the cheek. I haven't seen her since Jake's wedding, and in my quest to convince Blair to spend time with me, I've blown off a few dates with my sis.

"I'm sorry. I know I've been MIA."

"I've missed you! What's been keeping you so busy?"

"Let's go out back. I brought lunch. We can talk."

"Hmm." Sophia narrows her eyes and twists her mouth to the side, giving me her suspicious look. She knows me well.

For the last two weeks, I've been happier than ever before. After the Bethany fiasco, I convinced Blair to go to a Dodgers game, and we're taking it slow—although we've become more fluent at flirting via text, which leaves me so turned on that I'm ending my days with a fist around my cock.

I'm addicted to her. Yes, she's incredibly sexy, but I forgot how funny she can be, too. I'm desperate to get my hands on her body again. We've kept it PG and focused on learning more about one another. I love getting to know her all over again.

I lay out our favorite Chinese chicken salad from Joan's on Third and grab two waters from the kitchen.

"Spill it. Obviously, you have something big to tell me. Should I be nervous?"

I know Sophia won't care that I'm seeing Blair, but I want to be respectful of the relationship they have, too. She should know what's going on with us. Even if I'm not a hundred percent sure if we are officially an "us."

"So, Blair..." I clear my throat. I'm nervous. I didn't tell Blair that I was letting Sophia know about us, and now I'm having second thoughts. Maybe I should have talked to her first.

"What about Blair?" Sophia has a huge smile on her face as she takes a big bite of her salad.

"I was going to say that we've been spending more time together...in a non-professional capacity."

"Smother Pucker. I knew it."

"I wanted to make sure you were ok with this."

She snaps her head back up to look at me. "Of course I'm ok! I love this!"

"How are you feeling about signing with her?"

"I think she's the one for me. She's already set me up to meet with Grant after Labor Day about a project I'm in love with. She said she'd go with me even if I don't sign with her. Classy."

I roll my eyes at the mention of Grant. I'm still not

convinced he isn't interested in Blair. And he's way too old for my sister.

"I'm sure Grant can't wait to meet with both of you."

"What's that?" Sophia points her fork at me.

"What?"

"You're jealous."

Fuck yeah, I'm jealous.

"I can see you thinking. You are totally jealous."

I roll my eyes and stand to clear off the table. It's my cue to Sophia that it's time to wrap up this visit and get back to work.

"Did you have a chance to look at the contract Blair sent over?" Sophia asks me.

I hesitate because I've had an idea brewing but it could blow up in my face. I don't think Sophia should sign with Blair right now with the uncertainty of TWA and her name on a list of departures. But I can't really suggest it without context, and both Sophia and Blair will want to know why.

"I haven't yet," I say, "but I will."

"Thank you, big brother."

"Soph... Do you think..."

"Spit it out."

"Nothing. I was just thinking about how it might be better timing to sign once this TWA merger is done."

"You think I should wait?"

"I think you should trust your instincts. If you feel good about Blair, sign."

Sophia gives me a look that says she knows better. "I think you are working on this merger and you know something you can't tell me."

I wrap my sister in a quick hug and promise to send her over some options for dinner next week, but she doesn't let our conversation go just yet.

"Maybe you need a little more time to review the contract?" she asks. The undertone of that question tells me that she understands what I'm suggesting.

"Yeah, maybe."

She nods, and I take off before she can question me anymore. I've already said too much, and Blair would kill me if she found out I was influencing Sophia's decision in the slightest.

On my drive back to the office, I think more about Blair. I definitely don't want anyone else touching her. I don't think she is seeing anyone else. I just assumed that since we were hanging out so much, she wouldn't have time for anyone else, but now I need to know for sure.

As I pull into my office, I realize that I'm fucked.

I am totally jealous, and I don't want Blair to be with anyone but me. The idea that she might be interested in someone else makes my heart feel like someone has reached in and wrapped their fingers around it and is squeezing it as tightly as possible.

The last two weeks have been so easy and fun. I crave time with her, even if it doesn't end in sex. I also dream about having sex with her every time I leave her. I'm so desperate for her that I didn't even realize I've been taking whatever I can get from her.

We need to talk.

I'm nervous even thinking those words. Those are relationship words, and I have no idea how to have a relationship with anyone.

Even worse, what if she doesn't want a relationship with me?

I text Blair to see if she's up for dinner tonight. I wait to see her response before I suggest a place.

ME

Dinner?

BLAIR

Sure. Time? Place?

ME

7pm

ME

My house?

I see three dots appear, then disappear, and then appear again. I jump in with another text so she doesn't think I'm suggesting this just to sleep with her.

ME

I wanted to cook for you. I make a mean lobster roll.

After a few more minutes, she responds.

BLAIR

Ok. Send me the address.

I text her my address and then jump into work so I can wrap things up here and get ready for tonight. Because I do not know what I'm going to say.

thirty-two

· · ·

BLAIR

WYATT'S PLACE IS BREATHTAKING. It's a house on the Santa Monica-Venice border with breathtaking views of the ocean. There is as much outdoor space as there is indoor space. It's an open floor plan with the living, dining, and kitchen areas all visible once you are inside. The back of the house is made of glass doors that slide open to a back patio. I notice the small spa connected to a gorgeous square pool and wonder if Bethany has been in there. Fences line the sides of the yard but not the back because it leads straight out onto the beach.

"This place is incredible." I'm standing at the open doors, looking out at the ocean while he's in the kitchen, working on dinner.

"Thanks. It's the one place that brings me peace."

"I can imagine the entertaining you must do here." How many women has he been able to seduce with this setup? Already, my panties are dropping, and I haven't even gotten close to him yet.

"Oh, I haven't really entertained yet. I've only lived here for a year. Unless you count Mom and Sophia. I guess a few buddies have come over to watch a game or two."

"Uh-huh. I can imagine the ladies are impressed."

"I don't know. Are you? You're the first lady I've ever invited here."

I stare at him, doing my best impression of not looking surprised. Then I nod and try to change the subject as I walk over to the kitchen island.

"So, lobster rolls, yeah?"

"I went home with Jake one summer. He's from Connecticut, and we used to eat at this place on Sea Bluff Beach that only had three things on the menu: lobster rolls, lobster chowder, and lobster salad. To this day, I dream about that lobster roll and have worked hard to recreate it," He laughs as he tells the story.

The last two weeks have been almost too perfect. We've been spending more time together, and I'm finding it hard to remember why I should stay away from him. We slipped right back into the comfort and banter we had the first time we were together. It's almost as if no time has passed, except now we talk about work and clients instead of school, parents, or friends. When I'm with him, I forget about heartache. I forget I could get hurt again and that I need to be careful.

"Want to eat outside?"

"It feels like the right thing to do," I say.

He carries the food while I grab the glasses and a bottle of wine he's set out for us, and we walk over to a table near the end of the patio, steps away from the sand. It's a little windy out, but tonight is warmer than normal, the perfect temperature to dine outside.

When I sit down, I notice the balcony above, and Wyatt turns his head to see what I'm looking at.

"There's a fire pit up there. We can check it out after dinner."

He catches my eyes and holds them for a minute. I don't say anything because I don't want to ruin what could be a moment. I'd definitely like to go upstairs.

"Sounds nice."

Dinner is messy but delicious. He tells me what it was like to go to UCLA, and I share my stories about grad school at Stanford and why I changed my mind about practicing law. It was just so boring. He laughs and agrees, but he's good at what he does. As much as he was born to golf, he was meant to be a lawyer, too.

We talk about Hollywood and the crazy clients we've had and then compare notes on some of the popular actors we both know, agreeing on who is a class act and who is appalling. We also laugh at how delusional it can get sometimes when studios are trying to make deals and act as if life will cease to exist if they can't agree with a director over how an explosion scene should play out.

We never seem to run out of things to talk about, and I imagine what it might be like if this were something more. We know we have chemistry. I just can't tell if it's excitement I feel, or terror. Maybe it's both.

"So, I wanted to ask you something." He reaches across the table and threads his fingers through mine. "I know this is new, I know we're still figuring things out, but I guess I just wanted to know what you're thinking?"

I'm not sure what he wants me to say. I'm thinking I want to be with him. I want to spend the night with him. And I'm for sure thinking I don't ever want him to see that Bethany woman again. "What are you thinking?"

"I'm thinking I don't want to be with anyone else. Do you?"

I rub my thumb inside the palm of his hand. "No, I don't." And that's true, I don't want to be with anyone else. But I'm still hanging on to a little fear. Wyatt must see that in my eyes.

"I'm not saying we have to declare our love for one another, but while we're figuring out what we are, I'd like us to be exclusive. No other people. Just me and you."

"No Bethany?"

"Definitely no Bethany. Only you."

He brings my hand to his lips, dusting a light kiss over my knuckles. He pulls me up and over to sit on his lap. Our eyes connect, a million declarations left unsaid for now. I lean in for a taste of his lips and he tightens his arms around my waist as if confirming our pact. His teeth nip at my bottom lip as he pulls back, still holding me close.

"Let me put the dishes up, and then we can take our glasses upstairs and finish this bottle of wine by the fire," he whispers.

I help him clear the table and watch as he pushes up his shirt sleeves so he can rinse the dishes off before putting them in the dishwasher. His forearms flex, showcasing their ropey veins and muscles and drawing my eyes down to his hands.

They are strong, and his fingers are long, with perfectly mani-
cured nails. I get distracted thinking about those hands on my
body. They make me feel small and adored.

"You ok?"

I snap my eyes up to see that Wyatt has caught me staring
at him, and I blush.

"Yes, just thinking about some calls I need to make
tomorrow."

He smiles at me like he knows I'm full of shit. "Come on.
Let's go up."

Wyatt motions for me to lead the way. At the top of the
stairs, I'm met with another wall of glass doors, leading out to
a smaller patio with a round firepit and four Adirondack
chairs. There's also a row of chaise lounge chairs facing the
unobstructed view of the ocean.

"This is so beautiful," I say. "If I lived here, I don't think I
would ever come inside. I would sleep on those lounge chairs
and work all day around the fire pit."

Wyatt smiles at me and threads his fingers through mine
as he pulls me outside.

He leads us over to the lounge chairs and pushes two of
them together. Then he pulls a small table to the side of one
of the lounge chairs so we have a place for our wine and
glasses. I want to say something sarcastic about his boldness
connecting the chairs, but I can't because my mouth is totally
dry, and my thighs clench together in hopes those chairs see
some inappropriate action soon.

He climbs onto one lounge and stretches out with his
shirt untucked and bare feet crossed at the ankles. Then he
pats the other seat for me to join him. I sit, but my heart is

racing, and I'm worried that if I get too close to him, he'll hear it.

"I'm really glad you came over tonight." Wyatt turns on his side to face me, propping his head up with his arm. He brushes a strand of hair away from my lips.

"Me, too."

He leans close, and I can feel his breath on my lips. When he's this close, I just want to breathe in his scent.

"Stay the night with me, Blair."

"Ok."

He kisses me, pushing his tongue into my mouth, finding mine. The man can kiss. His hand reaches up to my neck, and then his fingers tangle in my hair to guide my head to a position where he can run his tongue along my neck.

"You are so beautiful. I've wanted to kiss you all week."

I bring my hands to the hem of his shirt, already wanting to take his clothes off. He grabs the back of his collar and pulls the shirt over his head. My eyes linger on the firmness of his chest and the definition of his abs, which seem to become more prominent with every turn of his body. He's so gorgeous. I missed touching him.

He puts his hands under the hem of my shirt. "Take this off."

I sit up and remove my shirt, and Wyatt looks at my body like he's obsessed. His are the only eyes that ever made me feel adored. He crawls on top of me, and I open my legs so he can settle between them. His hands brush my hair away from my face and his eyes linger for a moment, as if he's trying to memorize every eyelash, the curve of my cheeks, and pout of my lips.

He brings his mouth down to my chest, and kisses me over the top of my bra. His hands come up over my breasts, and his thumb teases my nipple. I thrust my hips into him in response. I can feel how hard he is for me already, and it makes me feel powerful that I have that effect on him.

"Be careful, Blair. You keep twisting those hips into me, and I'm going to rip your jeans off and show you how hard you've made me."

I'm greedy, so I push into him again. I want to feel him inside me.

He groans as he slides down and kisses my belly. Then he moves further down my body so his mouth is at the top of my jeans.

"I want to make you feel good. I want to taste you. I want you to come on my tongue, and then I want to fuck you until you come again."

I'm breathing so hard that all I can do is nod.

"How does that sound?"

"It...it sounds good."

Wyatt smirks as he unbuttons my jeans and pulls them off. He traces my panties with his fingers and pushes them to the side. Then he slides his middle finger down my slit and pushes it inside.

"You are soaking wet, Blair. Do you like my hands on you?"

"Yes," I whisper.

He grabs my panties and slides them off. Then he kisses the inside of my thighs, once, then twice, and swipes his tongue up the length of my pussy, causing me to cry out in pleasure.

I can feel him smile against me, and he teases me with his tongue and fingers. It doesn't take long before I'm close. He already owns my body.

"I love how responsive you are. It drives me crazy."

Wyatt sucks hard on my clit, and I fall over with what has to be one of the best orgasms I've ever had. He crawls up my body, kissing me along the way.

"You taste delicious."

I'm overwhelmed with how I'm feeling and instantly want more. He gives me a confidence I haven't felt with other men, taking his time scanning my body like he's trying to memorize every curve and valley. He makes me feel beautiful and wanted.

"I want to feel you inside me now, Wyatt."

I reach for him and realize he's still wearing his jeans. He leans back on his knees, and I sit up to help him get undressed. The moment his cock springs free, I can't help but reach for it—I haven't spent any time with it face to face—but as I lean forward to put it in my mouth, Wyatt tries to stop me.

"You don't have to."

I look up at him. "I want to."

I push him down on the chaise so I can position myself over him and run my tongue along his cock as I wrap my hand around him. Teasing the tip with my tongue, I lick away the precum leaking out and then wrap my lips around and take him inside my mouth.

"Jesus, fuck, Blair. That feels so good."

He looks down at me and brings his hands to my hair to hold it back so he can see my face.

As I take him as far back as I can, I can tell he wants to guide me but is holding back. I slide back and forth while his hands gently move my head to pace me.

Wyatt pulls me off of him so fast that it takes me a minute to realize what's happening. "I need to be in you now."

He reaches for his jeans, pulls out a condom, and slides it on. "I don't know if I'll be able to hold back. I want you so much. You tell me if it's too much. I don't want to hurt you."

"Please don't hold back. I want all of you, Wyatt."

He slides in fast with one deep push, and I gasp.

"Ok?"

I nod. "Keep going."

He pounds into me hard and deliberately, like he's trying to reach as far inside my soul as he can. I push my hips back into him and feel him hit a place deep inside that begins to unravel me. He lifts my leg, moving my ankle over his shoulder for deeper access, and I can't help but moan out his name.

"I want you to come again before I do."

"Wyatt."

I say his name like a plea. And it is. Underneath is me begging him not to stop. Begging him to never let me go. Begging him to love me. Because, as much as I fight it, I know I love him.

He reaches down to touch me, and I explode again. His pace picks up and then I feel his release as he comes undone. We're both out of breath as he kisses my neck and then my jaw, eventually ending up at my lips.

"Are you ok? Was it too much?"

"It was perfect."

He kisses down my neck and over my breasts, swirling his tongue around my nipples. My body heats at the same time that a shiver travels up my spine. He licks back up my neck and savors my lips a moment more before lifting his body off mine.

"I'll be right back." He gets rid of the condom and returns with a washcloth. After we clean up, he grabs a blanket and covers us as he lays back down, pulling me close to him so that our naked bodies are wrapped together. His arm moves around my shoulders so his fingers can run through my hair.

"I hope your neighbors enjoyed the show," I say.

"Nah. You can't see anything from the sides of the house. But if anyone was on the beach and looked up, they may have gotten more than they bargained for."

I tuck my head against his chest, unable to stop the laughter that escapes. This is about the time I'd normally panic, but right now, all I can think about is how comfortable I feel in his arms.

thirty-three

. . .

WYATT

I WAKE up to Blair's arms and legs wrapped around my body, and it feels like home. I like how she looks in my bed, and I have this powerful urge to never let her leave. Last night, we felt like more. It felt serious.

She stirs and slowly opens her eyes, and when she finds mine, she gives me a little smile.

"What time is it?" she asks. She stretches a little but doesn't untangle herself from me.

"Just after seven a.m." I'm growing hard against her naked body. I can't get enough of her.

"I need to get going. I have a ten a.m. meeting."

As I kiss down her neck, my hands find her breasts. "You're naked," I say.

"So are you."

The corners of her mouth twitch upwards, and she tries to hide her face in my neck. Her hands slide down my back as she pulls her body closer to mine. I cover her mouth with mine and push her back into the bed. Then I roll over her, place my arms to frame her head, and stare down at her. She is so gorgeous that it takes my breath away.

"You're going to make me late, sir."

"I'll make it worth your time."

She pulls me to her lips and flicks her tongue into my mouth, claiming mine.

I grab a condom off the nightstand and after I slip it on, I sink into her, both of us lost in each other. When our eyes lock, we both fall apart together.

"I enjoy waking up with you in my bed," I tell her as I kiss the corner of her lip.

"I do, too," she whispers.

"You ok?" I ask.

She nods, holds my face with both hands, and kisses me tenderly. I deepen the kiss, wishing that I could stay in bed with her all day. Then I drag her out of bed and to the bathroom.

I start the shower and pull her into the water with me. With my arms around her, I let the warmth of the stream run over her back.

She turns to face the water and runs her hands over her hair, getting it wet. I reach for my body wash so I can lather up her body.

"I only have my shampoo and body wash in here. I'm sorry. I should have thought ahead."

"It's ok. I enjoy knowing you have nothing in here for women. And I kind of like how you smell. I'll have your scent on me all day."

I kiss her again, and then we finish washing one another and rush to get dressed.

"Will I see you at the office?" Blair asks me.

"Not today. I'm meeting with my father to go over some last details on the merger docs. Can I see you later this evening?"

I feel guilty that I haven't told Blair what's happening at TWA. This is the only reason I could imagine keeping things professional, so I don't feel like I'm totally betraying her trust. Nothing is set in stone yet, so I'll see how everything shakes out, but if her name is on the final documents, I have to tell her. I don't want her to be blindsided. Thankfully, we have a little time.

"I have dinner with Naomi tonight, but I'll call you when I get home."

We walk out together and enjoy one last lingering kiss before we get into our separate cars and head to work.

I'm still smiling when I get to the office. The memory of Blair in my bed last night and this morning plays on a loop in my mind, and I feel like nothing can bring me down today. With any luck, I can convince her my bed is a place she should always be. Or her bed, too. I believe in equality.

As I walk into my dad's office, the usual air of authority hangs in the room. He barely looks up from his papers.

"Hey, Wyatt. What's the latest with the TWA merger? I saw Blair's name on the layoff list. Is that going to be an issue?" His tone is as casual as ever, like he didn't just throw a grenade into my chest.

"No, it won't be an issue. Everything's under control," I reply, trying to keep my voice steady.

"Good," he says, finally looking at me with a piercing

stare. "It's important to keep things professional, especially now. You know better than to cross any lines."

I swallow hard as the guilt settles like a rock in my stomach. "I'm aware. I've got it handled."

His eyes narrow. "Wyatt, I hope you're not getting distracted again. Blair's a pleasant woman, but this is business. We can't afford any complications."

There it was, the lecture I'd been dreading. My jaw tics as frustration bubbles up.

"I understand the stakes," I say, forcing the words out, careful not to make any promises I won't be able to keep.

He gives me a curt nod, and his expression remains hard. "Just remember, you're part of this team. We have responsibilities to our clients and the firm. Don't let personal feelings overrule logic again."

I nod as the weight of his words press down on me. "Understood."

I leave his office and head to my own, feeling trapped between duty and desire. Blair's impending layoff is burning a hole in my conscience, and it's inevitable that I will disappoint someone.

A knock startles me, and I'm surprised to see Jake in my doorway. I thought he was supposed to be on his honeymoon for a few more days. He and Lauren were supposed to spend a month in Italy.

"Why are you here?"

"Can't a guy just come visit his friend?"

"Sure, but that friend is supposed to be on his honeymoon."

Jake slides his hand down his face, and I see the exhaustion peek through. "Lauren wanted to come back for some *Housewives* casting call."

"What?"

"Don't."

I raise my hands in surrender and do what I can to be supportive. "Well, if it makes you feel any better, I just stepped into the biggest conflict of interest shitshow."

"Looks like I got here just in time."

Normally I would push Jake more, but I can see that he's trying to work out how he feels right now, and I could use his advice. "It's the TWA work."

"I thought you were excited about that? I mean, you won't come work with me, so I thought taking on this account was the next best thing?"

"It is, but it's kind of interfering with my personal life."

"Hmm," Jake raises an eyebrow, waiting for me to say more before he decides how to respond to that.

"I'm kind of seeing Blair, but nobody knows it. Well, Sophia does. And maybe Blair's friend Jess. And now you. But it's new, and we haven't even labeled it or anything."

"Well, don't fuck it up, then," Jake says with a hearty laugh.

"I'm trying not to." I let a small laugh escape, too.

I explain how Blair was initially part of the meetings and involved in everything that was happening at TWA but then Lance cut her out. I didn't really think anything of it, and it actually made it easier for us to entertain the possibility of rekindling our feelings for one another. But then a few suggestions I made to help cut costs inadvertently put Blair at the top of a layoff list.

"And she has no idea?"

"No. In fact, I think she thinks if she signs Sophia, she's protected and safe."

"You can't let Sophia sign with her, then."

"I know. I'm trying to figure that out, too. Fuck. How did I go from finally getting everything I want to fucking it all up at the same time?"

"Sorry, man. Can you tell her?"

"Not right now. I'd feel better about telling her if we were close to the notification date and her name on the list was for sure final. But until then, I can't say anything."

"Maybe it's time for work to keep you really busy right now."

I know what he's implying: that I keep my distance so I'm not tempted to share confidential information. But the last time I kept my distance it backfired in the grandest of ways. And I'm not sure I can stay away, even if I should.

thirty-four

. . .

BLAIR

NOT EVEN LANCE can ruin my mood today. He's already come by twice, asking questions about Sophia. I've never seen him this pushy about getting updates on talent. I left a message, hoping to catch up with her sometime this week. I didn't tell Lance she has a contract in her hands and I'm just waiting for a signature.

I know I'm the right agent for her, and I know she likes what I can offer and what I will fight for as her agent. I know she wanted Wyatt to review terms, but well, he has been a little preoccupied.

I don't realize I'm smiling until Stella comes in to let me know it's time to go meet Naomi.

"What's got you so happy today?" she asks.

I look around her at the open door to see if anyone's within earshot.

"Wyatt."

"Spill it! Tell me what is going on!" She shuts my office door and heads over to the couch.

I'm filling her in on dinner and the sleepover when Stella interrupts. "Hang on. I'm dialing in Jess. Unless you've already told her?" she asks as she dials.

"Good idea. I have four texts I haven't responded to."

"Your hands better have been tied up, and your mouth full of something inappropriate!" Jess yells through the phone. "It's the only excuse I'll accept for leaving me on read!"

"I think it is her excuse!" Stella says. "You're on speaker, and Blair is about to recap last night's sexy time with Wyatt!"

I give them the play-by-play, doing my best to sidestep the crude questions from Jess. Poor Stella. She didn't ask for a sex education course, but you're guaranteed to learn a new kink every time Jess is around.

As I continue, I realize that I'm not sure how to define what Wyatt and I are just yet. It seems way too fast to just jump into something serious, but I also don't want to see anyone else either. Situationship has never made more sense than right now.

"Do you think he wants to date you?" Stella asks.

"It doesn't matter what he wants," Jess says. "What does Blair want?"

"It kinda matters what he wants," I say.

"Don't worry about labeling anything right now," Jess says. "You need to sleep with him a few more times, make sure that chemistry is real and you're not holding on to some past perception of who you think he is."

"I don't think I could move forward without labeling it," Stella says quietly.

But Jess is right. How much of what I feel is based on the

past? Are memories driving desire? I'm finally learning who present-day Wyatt is, but it's still early. What I know for sure is that I want to see him again. If I didn't have this dinner with Naomi tonight, I'd probably invite him over.

I promise to keep both Stella and Jess updated on the progress and then head over to The Front Yard, a little hole-in-the-wall restaurant next to The Garland Hotel in Studio City. I see Naomi instantly and rush to wrap my arms around her. Even though our offices are on the same floor, our rosters are so different that we barely see each other.

"You look fucking incredible! And happy! What's new?" Naomi asks.

We sit and let the server know we'll both have a chardonnay and water before I return the compliment. "You look gorgeous—like always. And I'm kind of seeing someone."

"You flatter me. I need to spend more time with you! Now, tell me everything!"

Naomi looks like a runway model: large almond eyes that are light yellowish brown, eyelashes that look fake but aren't, high cheekbones, full, heart-shaped lips, and a straight, perfectly buttoned nose. Her skin is creamy tan and flawless. She looks like she spent hours putting on makeup, but her coloring and features just give the appearance of elegance. She doesn't wear much makeup at all.

"Seriously," I say, "what is that dress you are wearing? It hugs your body in all the right places. You look incredible."

"Oh, this old thing?" Naomi laughs, but I can tell she's thrilled to get the compliment. "Girl, it's the Spanx Perfect Sheath Dress. It holds me in all the right places!"

"Sara Blakely continues to do the Lord's work. That's for sure."

We laugh and make small talk while we glance at the menus and pretend we might order something other than the salad, but we both opt for the winter grains salad with salmon.

"So, spill. Who's the guy? And what's the latest with Sophia?"

"Contract is with Sophia. It's almost done. And the guy... well, it's her brother. Wyatt. The attorney helping with the merger."

"I thought you were just friends?" She teases. "Start from the beginning."

I tell her the movie version of our story, how we had a brief fling in high school, lost touch when we left for college, and reconnected when I went to meet Sophia for the first time.

"So, did you know Sophia was his sister?"

"Not at first. Once I started due diligence on her, I realized Sophia Ford is actually Sophia Bradford. But I'm not sure I would've even connected the dots then. She was in junior high when we were seniors, and I didn't really know her, much less that she was an aspiring actress."

"I love this story! So, is it serious?"

"It's new. That's all I can say with confidence at this point."

"Fair enough, but I want updates. Don't leave me hanging on this."

"I promise. What about you? I haven't seen you around lately."

We both stop talking when our food arrives. It's a small town, and ears are everywhere. Once our server leaves, Naomi drops the bomb.

"I'm thinking about leaving TWA."

"What? Why?" I ask.

"Eh, I'm sleeping with Lance. Well, I was. As of about an hour ago, I'm not anymore."

I'm not sure anything could have shocked me more. Not only is it an unlikely match-up, but I thought Lance was married.

She must see the look of shock on my face because she says, "He's not married anymore, but I'd be lying if I said this didn't start before his divorce was final."

"So, is the affair over because you are leaving? Or are you leaving because the affair is over?"

"The affair is over because he started sleeping with my assistant. I'm leaving because I need a change of scenery. It would be weird to stay, I'm sure, but I'm just not challenged anymore."

"I can relate to that," I tell her as my mind drifts to the last few times Lance shut down my ideas.

"If I'm lucky, they'll add my name to the list of layoffs and just package me out. That would be the ideal scenario. Then I'll be paid to go on vacation and take a breather while I figure out my next move."

"What layoff list?" I ask.

"For the merger. They have to look cash-flow positive before everything is signed, sealed, and delivered. Word around the office is Lance just wants to cut headcount to make the budget work. I thought you, of all people, would know this."

"Why would I know?"

"Aren't you in all of those meetings? And Wyatt, too?"

"I'm not anymore," I tell her. "Lance said I was no longer needed. I'm guessing that's why."

I get an uneasy feeling. Jess mentioned layoffs, too, but it's been quiet around the office, and Wyatt hasn't said a thing about it, either. Not that he would.

"Promise me you'll let me know if you hear anything," Naomi says.

"Of course. Same to you."

We shift topics to the latest on-set gossip, but I have a hard time focusing on the rest of our dinner. All I can think about is if Wyatt would tell me if my contract is in jeopardy or if he would not mention it at all under the guise of professionalism.

thirty-five

. . .

WYATT

I'M BACK in the TWA offices and stop by Blair's office to surprise her with her favorite coffee from Caffe Luxxe before I join Lance and the rest of the team for meetings that will last all day.

My heart rate speeds up when I see her, and my hands twitch with the desire to touch her. She's so fucking gorgeous in a black pencil skirt and a basic white button-down shirt. She's wearing those damn heels again. I swear I will fuck her with only those shoes on at some point. She's pulled her hair back today; it makes her look like a sexy librarian, and the stir in my pants agrees.

She looks happy to see me, so I shut her door to give us a moment of privacy.

"I didn't know you were coming by!"

I wrap my arms around her waist and rest my chin on top of her head, breathing in that citrus and vanilla scent I love so much before giving her a quick kiss.

"I took a chance you might want a coffee."

"I love this place! How did you know?"

"I didn't, but it seemed like a place you would like."

The look she gives me makes me want to confess that I'm ready to move her into my house. We can have our wedding out on the beach and live happily ever after. Kids negotiable.

"How was dinner last night?" I ask. We exchanged a few texts, but between her late dinner and my working late to prove to my dad that I was taking this merger seriously, we didn't get to talk.

"It was great! Naomi mentioned something interesting, though."

She hesitates while I stay quiet. I give her time to decide whether she wants to confide in me.

"She said TWA is going to lay off a ton of staff to hit targets before the deal closes."

Blair keeps her eyes latched on mine with a look that says she won't ask me directly but she wants me to tell her what I know. It takes every bit of restraint to keep my face neutral. It's not the time or place to have this conversation. I don't want to lie to her, but I'm not ready to tell her anything.

"So, how long have you and Naomi worked together?"

"Oh, gosh, almost five years now. She moved to LA from NY but arrived fully connected in this town."

"Do you guys hang out much?"

"Ok, message received. You're going to be late for your meeting," she says. Her eyes narrow in suspicion, so I lean in, hoping a kiss will distract her.

"Have dinner with me tonight?"

"Fine. But let's order in. You come to my place."

She runs her hands down my chest, smoothing over my

shirt. She's avoiding my gaze, and I can tell she's disappointed by the direction of the conversation. I just need her to trust me for a few days, and then she'll understand why I couldn't say more now.

"I should be done by six, and then I'll head over," I tell her as I lean in for one last kiss.

When I open Blair's door, I almost run into Lance, and the irritated look on his face rivals the guilty shock on mine.

"Wyatt," he says, "I didn't know you were already in the office."

"He had some questions on behalf of Sophia. He's helping her review a proposal I've given her," Blair says as she steps up behind me to play out the excuse.

"That sounds promising," Lance says.

"I'll connect with Sophia and have her reach out," I tell Blair with a nod and exit her office.

"Hang on, Wyatt. I'll walk over to the conference room with you."

I give Blair a quick look, and she responds with the slightest shake of her head, implying that I should say nothing —about us, Sophia, or something else; I'm not exactly sure.

As we walk away, Lance clamps his hand on my shoulder and leans in close to my ear. "I hope your relationship with Blair will not be a problem," he whispers.

"I'm not sure I understand what you mean."

"I think you do." He slaps his hand on my shoulder and walks over to greet everyone in the conference room.

After finding me in Blair's office, Lance is relentless with the meetings all day. He's usually the first one to ditch, but today, he stays for every single one and does his best to ensure they last as long as possible. I barely have time to check in with Blair, and lunch is a granola bar from the basket of snacks on the credenza in the room.

The meetings continue into the late afternoon. At the rate we're going, I'll be lucky to finish here by six, so I reach for my phone to give Blair a heads-up.

ME

Hey, still here. Not sure we'll wrap by six.

BLAIR

I'm sorry. Lance can be a dick. Just come over when you're done.

ME

Ok, I'll let you know when I'm on the way.

"Wyatt, have you reviewed all the contract language and the notification messaging?"

I look up to see Lance glaring across the table. I already shared earlier that I reviewed all the documents and nothing raised any red flags. "Yes, we're all good there."

I don't know why he keeps staring at me with such irritation. Ever since he saw me in Blair's office, he's been acting as if I've spoiled some grand plan. I worry for a minute that the hypothetical executive having an affair has something to do with him and Blair.

ME

You and Lance...anything ever happen between you two?

BLAIR

Are you kidding me?

ME

Definitely been a shift in his behavior since seeing me in your office.

ME

Maybe he has a crush?

BLAIR

No chance.

ME

You never know.

BLAIR

Believe me, I know.

BLAIR

Watch your back, though. He's evil. And if he's being a dick, there's something he's not happy about.

ME

Great.

As predicted, Lance keeps us throughout dinner, but at least he has the decency to order in food for everyone. As I drop my trash into the bin out in the hallway, I hear him call out my name.

"Hey, great work today. I really appreciate everything you are doing. I can't tell you what an asset you've been to our team."

I turn my head to look at his hand, which is back on my shoulder again. This must be a tell of his, a move that says, *I don't fucking like what is going on, but I'm not sure what is going on, so I'll play along with a friendly grip on your shoulder.*

"I'm glad to hear it."

"Yeah, I was just speaking with your father. I wanted to make sure that we're all good." Lance offers me his best display of his twinkling white veneers.

I'm confused. I'm not sure what he would be talking to my father about. He must see it on my face.

"You know. That your relationship with Blair won't be a problem. He let me know about your history with her and assured me that your priority is TWA. In fact, he was surprised to hear you were still talking to her. I explained our offices are on the same floor so you two were bound to run into one another."

As if on cue, my phone buzzes in my pocket, and I don't even have to guess who it is. I know it's my father. And I already know he is livid that Lance called him.

"He's absolutely right. My relationship with Blair is strictly professional," I say through clenched teeth, unable to calm the rage running through my veins.

"And you'll let me know any updates on Sophia's proposal?" Lance says.

Everything is becoming super clear now. He knows Sophia wants Blair and, if Blair can lock her in before she's terminated, it will be a year before Sophia can renegotiate with TWA unless she agrees to a huge penalty payment.

"I'm sure Blair will keep you updated. That's really not my place."

"But it's your place to review a proposal from TWA, or Blair, actually?" Lance says. The question is rhetorical, and the subtext is that I need to prove my professionalism.

"We better get back in there." I walk away before I lose control and tell that cocksucker to fuck off.

When we finally wrap for the evening, I'm too in my head to go to Blair's house, so I head home. I feel like an asshole when I finally text her a few hours later with the lie that we've just wrapped. I'm hoping that she's already in bed, but when she responds, I pile on to an already shitty day by telling her an even shittier lie.

BLAIR

I'm still awake. I can have a glass of whisky waiting for you.

ME

I better not. Lance sent me away with homework I need to finish by tomorrow. Raincheck?

BLAIR

Of course. I'm sorry you had a shit day.

I don't respond to her because I'm that big of a dick. I need some time to figure out how I want to handle this.

thirty-six

· · ·

BLAIR

I HAVEN'T SEEN Wyatt in four days, and I miss him. I hate that I miss him, too. I'm swinging between trying to understand that he's busy with work and feeling like this is déjà vu.

I get a twinge in my gut that something is off here. I've been giving Wyatt space because what he's focused on is confidential. As much as I want him to share what's going on, he can't. I wonder if he's feeling stressed. I rub my hand across my forehead, and the tension sinks into my shoulders.

ME

> Free for lunch today? I hear you'll be nearby

WYATT

> I wish! At my office today. Lance rescheduled today's meetings.

I try not to let the disappointment come through my next message. Thank God he can't see my face right now.

I hate how fake and cheerful I sound. Technically, I have no reason to be upset. It's my insecurities trying to sabotage me. I grab my purse and text Jess to meet me down the street for lunch. I need to process.

I grab a table on the patio, and I can tell I'm in a terrible mood when I look up and immediately feel angry about how great Jess looks. It's not fair how flawless and naturally beautiful she is. She's wearing black joggers, her panda Nike dunks, and a black sports bra with a tan trench coat over it all. Her hair is tied in a loose ponytail, and she's only wearing a little mascara and lip gloss, but she looks like she stepped out of the pages of a magazine.

"It's so unfair how hot you look."

"Someone's in a mood." Jess pulls out a chair and grabs a sip from my wine glass as she sits down.

"I miss Wyatt."

"Easy. Call him." She smiles at me as she takes a bite of her pastry.

I roll my eyes and let out a huff. "I did. He keeps blowing me off."

"Say more." She digs into the bread as she looks around for our server.

"I had dinner with Naomi the other night, and she mentioned they are cutting a ton of staff at TWA before the deal closes."

"I told you!" She points at me.

"I think Wyatt knows something and is avoiding me so he

doesn't violate any attorney-client privilege. I think my name is on that list."

"Fuck, Blair. Really?"

"Lance has been extra about signing Sophia. He was weird about finding Wyatt in my office, and now Wyatt has ninety-nine excuses about why he can't see me. I'm definitely on the list."

"What are you going to do?"

"About Wyatt or the job?"

"Both."

"I can't even process the job part yet because nothing is real until it happens. But I'm afraid Wyatt is going to check out again." I'm trying not to panic and think he'll ditch me like he did before, but I don't really know how much power or influence his father has over him now. I know it was a big deal for Wyatt to get this assignment from his dad.

"Ok, then let's break this down." She leans in and puts her hands on my face, forcing me to breathe. "First, you're right. He can't tell you anything right now."

"I know." I hesitate before I admit this next part. "What if it's a mistake to trust him?"

We're interrupted by the server and then by Stella and Brandon as they walk by our table on their way to the coffee shop next door. We take a minute to say hi and catch up, and then Stella directs our attention across the street.

"Hey, isn't that Wyatt...and Lance?" she says.

I look over and see Wyatt entering a restaurant with Lance, and a feeling of irritation mixed with hurt floods through my body.

He totally lied to me.

"Yep," I say. "He mentioned Lance changed the meeting for today."

Technically, this is true. He just implied that there were no meetings today and that he wouldn't be anywhere near my office.

When Stella and Brandon leave, Jess questions my reaction to seeing Wyatt. I recap the story he gave me about his plans for today, which just reinforces my insecurities.

"If you aren't sure what's going on, just go talk to him," she says. "Don't let him blow you off. You're not in high school anymore."

I bring my thumbnail up to my mouth and gnaw on it, thinking about what she said.

She's right.

"Besides," she continues, "I've known since the Paley event that he is obsessed with you."

"Bullshit."

"Bullshit!" she yells back at me. "It was so obvious when you introduced us."

I want her to be right. I've been so focused on being cautious that I missed my heart leaping into love territory.

We finish the lunch by catching up on her life. There's always something exciting happening, and she's close to getting a super-exclusive interview that she can't tell me about yet. She promises I'll be shocked and impressed with the name. I'm always impressed with her.

As I walk back to the office, I know I have two calls to make. One is to Sophia. She needs to know that I have little confidence in my stability here at TWA and, if she wants to sign with me specifically, she should wait until we get through the rumored layoffs. If it's the backing of TWA she's looking for, I can set her up with the names of other agents I trust.

The second call is to Wyatt. It's time for another talk.

thirty-seven

. . .

WYATT

FUCK. I knew it was a bad idea to meet Lance near the TWA offices. When we sat down at our table, I spotted Blair across the street with Jess, and it looked like Stella and Brandon, too. There's no way she didn't see us walk in. My insides are twisting with nerves because even though I told her Lance had rescheduled, I intentionally misled her to think there were no meetings today and I would be nowhere near her offices.

I met Lance to talk through the details needed to wrap up the work around this merger. I wanted to confirm the specifics of the decisions TWA was moving forward with, like timing, impacts on employees, and next steps. The rest of the deal is mostly regulatory process, and I've set up the in-house legal team to manage it. They can reach out for any unique concerns or needs on an ad hoc basis.

I also wanted to let Lance know I wouldn't be coming back to the TWA offices. As much as I want to see Blair, working with her leadership on decisions that impact her directly has become a conflict of interest.

I've spent so many years avoiding relationships and intimacy. But I've always loved Blair. The realization hit me like a wave, powerful and undeniable. It's a truth I've buried deep, hidden behind career ambitions and family expectations, and now it's risen to the surface with a clarity I can't ignore. I want to pursue her, to be with her fully, and I'm willing to make the necessary changes in my life to do so. The connection we share now feels as deep as it was in high school, a bond that time and distance couldn't diminish. I hope she feels the same, that she sees the potential for us to be something more again.

Lance spent most of the lunch reminding me of my obligation to the NDA and my role of privilege. He knows damn well I'm going to tell Blair. I expect he'll reach out to my father about the whole thing. I'm not looking forward to that conversation, but it's going to have to wait. I have one more stop to make.

ME

Headed your way.

JAKE

Sounds good. We're all ready for you.

When I arrive at the Hays and Cole law firm, I'm greeted by an open reception area and a cheerful woman who's expecting me. She ushers me down the hall to one of the private conference rooms, letting me know there are refreshments inside.

I sit at the polished mahogany table. The rich scent of

leather-bound books and freshly brewed coffee fills the air. Ryan Cole and Matt Hays, the formidable duo behind one of the city's most prestigious entertainment law firms, sit across from me.

"We've been looking forward to this, Wyatt," Ryan begins, leaning forward with a smile that crinkles the corners of his eyes. "Jake's been singing your praises for years, and your reputation in the legal community speaks for itself."

Matt nods in agreement, his hands steepled in front of him. "Absolutely. We've wanted you to join us for a long time. Your expertise, particularly in contract negotiations and intellectual property, is exactly what we need to take Hays and Cole to the next level."

My heart pounds in my chest as a mixture of excitement and trepidation washes through me. This is my dream: to work with the best in the industry and carve out my legacy. Yet, the shadow of my father's expectations looms large.

"I can't tell you how much this means to me," I say, my voice steady despite the turmoil inside. "Joining your firm has always been a goal of mine, but I have to be upfront about the potential blowback. You know my father."

Ryan nods, and his gaze is sympathetic. "We understand, Wyatt. Family dynamics can be complicated. But we believe in you, and we're prepared to navigate any challenges that come our way."

Matt leans in and says in a reassuring tone, "Your father's firm is well respected, and we have no intention of causing any friction. We can keep this agreement confidential until you've had a chance to speak with him. The last thing we want is to put you in a difficult position."

I let out a breath I didn't realize I was holding. "Thank you. That means a lot. I just want to be sure that I'm worth the effort and potential risk for you."

Ryan smiles warmly. "We have no doubt about that, Wyatt. You've already proven your worth. Jake's endorsement alone speaks volumes, and we trust his judgment implicitly."

I nod, feeling a swell of gratitude and anticipation. "I appreciate your confidence in me. I promise to give this my all."

Ryan rises and extends his hand. "Welcome to Hays and Cole, Wyatt. We're thrilled to have you on board."

I stand and shake his hand and then Matt's. "Thank you. I won't let you down."

As I leave the office, my mind races with the possibilities ahead—as well as the challenges, the triumphs, and the conversation I need to have with my father. For the first time in a long while, I feel like I'm taking a step toward my future on my own terms, and it feels right.

thirty-eight

. . .

BLAIR

WHEN I SPOKE to Wyatt last night, I was afraid he was going to make another excuse to avoid me, but he asked me to meet him at his house for dinner tonight. Now I'm sitting in his driveway, unsure of what I'm going to say.

It's been twelve years since high school, twelve years since he hurt me, yet the connection we share now is undeniable. Despite my hesitation to trust him again, there's a bond between us that time hasn't erased. It feels like I'm losing control of my feelings, but at the same time, all I want is to drown in them. Wyatt makes me feel special. He makes me believe in forever.

He's the one person who truly understands me, who unconditionally supports my dreams and encourages me to reach higher. I've faced my fair share of men who felt threatened by my career. But not Wyatt. He's proud of my success, never intimidated.

But now he's been avoiding me, just like before, and a

nagging doubt makes me wonder if he feels the same way about me. I can't shake the feeling that he's hiding something about his work with my agency. In the past, he opted for the simple path instead of choosing what he wanted. Instead of choosing me. Now I need to know if I'm a priority for him or if I'm still not important enough.

We have a track record of avoiding each other when things get tough, so I'm here to confront him. He can't run away this time. I can't let him run away this time. We both deserve to know if we're worth fighting for.

His meeting with Lance has also stirred up some emotions that, apparently, I haven't faced. When I started at TWA, I was fresh out of law school and excited to help people chase their dreams of making it in Hollywood. It was so rewarding to read a script and know it was special. I loved to champion the underdog and find the hidden gems. It's how I was able to work my way up the agency's ladder so quickly.

People love stories. Storytelling is literally programmed into our DNA. When you dream in your sleep, that is your brain telling you stories. How about when a loved one is late for dinner? Do you think about why they might be late? Your brain is creating a story for you.

Knowing that we are hard-wired for stories, it's just a matter of what the world wants or needs to hear at this moment in time. It's basic psychology—and it's why I love meeting and reading and searching for the right projects and people to introduce to the world.

I thought hearing I might lose my job would be more devastating, but it's not. All I can think about is what it would be like to finally start my own agency. It would be a small shop. I'd be super selective about who we bring on and fully focused on trying to shift the narrative about women-led roles and stories.

The knock at my window startles me, and I see Wyatt smiling down at me.

"You going to sit out here all night?" he asks.

The look on his face is all it takes for my nerves to settle and my confidence returns. This is my guy. We can do this.

Moments later, as I stand in Wyatt's living room, the tension between us crackles like a live wire. I need to know where we stand. If he feels what I feel.

"You're avoiding me," I say. My voice is firm, but I'm trembling. "I can't keep pretending everything's fine. You're shutting me out again, and I won't go through that a second time."

Wyatt runs a hand through his hair, looking torn. "I know. I'm messing this all up. I need you to understand that I've been trying to protect you."

"I know about the layoffs," I say, stepping closer. "I suspect you saw my name on the list. Just be honest with me. Please."

He takes a deep breath, and his eyes lock onto mine. "You're right. I need you to know I intended to tell you everything, but I had to get a few things in order first."

"So, tell me everything."

"I'm under a strict NDA, but you are my priority. You're the only one who matters."

I feel a mix of relief and then concern.

"Don't risk your job. I get the gist of what's happening. And your father would be furious, I'm sure."

Wyatt steps forward, closing the distance between us. "I'm not worried about the job or my father. All I care about is you." His hand grips the back of my neck, and his thumb dusts over my lips.

"I told Lance today that I'm not returning to TWA. I'll wrap up the final details of this project, but then I'm passing the ongoing support to a colleague."

"Please tell me you didn't do this because of me," I say. "Please tell me you didn't back out of work I know you love just for me."

"Of course I did. But before you panic, I also accepted an offer from Hays and Cole. Nobody knows that yet. Not even my father."

I'm speechless. The shock must be apparent on my face.

"There's something else you should know," Wyatt says. He braces his hands around my face so my head is tilted up at him, as though he wants to make sure I hear his next words clearly.

"When I'm with you, I feel a peace I've only known one other time in my life. You make me feel like my dreams matter, like I matter. With us, I've never felt like I've had to be anyone except who I truly am. You inspire me to take risks I've always wanted to take and go after things I've always wanted. And I want you."

He seals his declaration with a kiss that sends fire through my body and sizzles every nerve in my heart. I wrap my arms around him and deepen the kiss, desperate to show him I'll always make him feel that way.

My heart pounds in my chest, a mixture of relief and fear, as he pulls back to look at how I'm taking this news.

"Wyatt, are you sure about this? About us?"

He nods, and his gaze is unwavering. "Blair, I clearly remember the day I met you. It changed my heart forever. I didn't understand what love was before that, and I didn't realize how good it would feel to have someone care for me, listen to me, accept, and want me, no matter my flaws. You gave me a second chance, and now I know for sure. You have my heart. It was always yours. It always will be."

As he pulls me into his arms, I feel the weight of the past twelve years lift off my shoulders. This time, we have a real chance. And I'm not going to let it slip away.

The stress and tension of the past few days, coupled with the admissions of our feelings, hit hard after dinner. Wyatt and I are both tired, and we should sleep, but we also can't keep our hands off each other.

"I need to shower. Care to join me?" Wyatt asks, already leading me toward his bathroom. I slowly unbutton my blouse, letting him know I'm interested. He turns on the water and when he turns back around I'm already pulling down my skirt and panties. I reach back to unsnap my bra, and watch his eyes follow its fall to the floor before they dart back up to linger over my naked body.

"Are you just going to stare? Or are you going to join me?"

He races to strip as I step into the steam and under the spray of the shower tilting my head back to soak my hair. He slides in against my body, and the warm water makes every-thing slick between us. His hands find my breasts and I lean into his touch, loving how strong his hands feel on my skin.

His thumb glides over my pebbled nipples and I can't stop the moan that escapes.

"Your hands feel so good."

My fingers explore his chest memorizing every curve of his hard body, while his lips find mine and his tongue tangles with mine. His hand grips the back of my neck pulling me closer as his other hand starts to travel down my side and around my back.

When he kisses me, the world fades away and everything I've ever wanted is right here. Every broken part, every scar, feels healed and complete. When I pull back, I see a flash of confusion cross his face, but right now, I want all of him. I want to make him feel treasured and loved the way he makes me feel. When I sink to my knees his eyes fill with adoration, desire, and need.

"You look fucking gorgeous on your knees."

I wrap my hand around him and glide my tongue along the length of him, circling around the tip and licking off the precum that is already leaking out of him. His hands gently caress my hair and I can feel him holding back, letting me control the pace.

"Look at me Blair. I want your eyes on me."

The moment our eyes connect, the world slips away and it's only us. This moment feels like more, like we're done with excuses and know there will never be anyone else for either of us. As I slide him into my mouth, I watch the ecstasy take over him.

"Jesus, fuck, Blair. So good."

I push my lips back down over him but he's big so I use

my hands to fill in the gap. He grunts like I'm torturing him and I can't help but smile.

"You like that? Like seeing how hard and crazy you make me?

His fingers twist in my hair and his grip grows tight on the sides of my head as he struggles to keep them still. My moan vibrates around him causing him to thrust hard against me, making me gag.

"Are you ok?"

I nod and keep going, taking him even deeper. Seeing him this turned on has me pressing my thighs together and I can feel my own hips tilting with need.

"God, Blair, your mouth is going to be the death of me. I'm so close."

I love how much I affect him. His head falls back and I can tell he's ready.

"I'm going to come. I want to come on your tits."

I pop off him and nod just as his release escapes and paints my chest. He's so gorgeous, and a feral look crosses his face as he admires his work.

He pulls me up and smashes his lips to mine kissing me like it's the end of the world. He breaks the kiss and glides his hands over my hair to move it back off my face.

"That was fucking hot. I had no idea how much I would enjoy seeing my cum all over you."

"Me either." I look down and run my fingers through the mess, a laugh tumbling out. "Good thing we're in the shower."

He kisses me again and then starts to lather my body up, taking care to clean every crease and crevice along the way.

It's a weird foreplay I didn't know would turn me on so much. I hope he knows that we're just going to get dirty all over again once we are out of here. I need more of him.

We dry off and slide into the sheets naked as he glides down my body to return the favor. And when he sinks into me after that, I dream of what our life could be like if this was our forever.

thirty-nine

. . .

WYATT

MY FATHER HASN'T MADE it in to work yet, but I know he won't hesitate to find me as soon as he arrives. I didn't respond to any of his messages last night, and it's obvious he's talked to Lance. The last message he left was a thinly veiled threat that if I were out with Blair, it would be an issue.

Blair and I didn't discuss specific details about what TWA is planning pre-merger, but I asked a lot of clarifying questions about her dreams and what she would do if she left TWA. She caught on to the subtext well enough, but I couldn't confirm the timing. That is something HR will work on with Lance. So, technically, no NDAs were broken, and no secrets are tripping up a second chance with Blair.

"Knock, knock," Sophia says as she walks through my open door. I hang on to the hug she gives me a little longer than normal.

"What's going on?" she asks. "You're clingy."

"I'm waiting for our father to get here so I can tell him I quit."

I've stunned her silent. Her eyes are wide, and her mouth breaks open to gasp, but no noise makes it out.

"I've accepted a position at Hays and Cole."

I lead her to my couch and give her a moment to recover.

"Dad is going to flip. Why? How? Are you ok?"

"More than ok. It's time. I never should have let him push me down a career path I didn't really want in the first place. It's always mentally fucked with me because I appreciate all he's done. I know how lucky I am to have the access and resources I do. But I've spent my whole life doing what he wants. It's ok for me to do what I want."

"This is big, Wyatt. I'm so proud of you. I am. Really. But..." She hesitates. "Are you sure?"

Sophia questioning my decision should irritate me, but it doesn't. I can see on her face that the concern is more about the backlash that will likely come from our father.

"This decision is a long time coming and is about more than just where I want to work," I say.

"Is this the part where you finally admit you're in love with Blair?"

I can't stop the smile that spreads across my face.

"Something like that. I'll just say that working at TWA is now a conflict of interest. The last time my career aspirations were tangled around someone I was in love with, I didn't make the right decision."

"I hate that he got in the way of your relationship back then."

"It's not all on him. I pulled back when he said she was selfish and didn't care about what was best for me. It didn't feel that way, but at the time, he was persuasive. I'm not blaming him totally. I know now that I should've trusted Blair enough to be honest with her. I won't make that mistake again. I've pre-empted any attempt he could make to incentivize me to stay here."

"No, you can't let him control your life. I understand, Wyatt."

She wraps her hand around mine and gives it a squeeze. A layer of concern still lies over the happiness I see on her face.

"So, my conversation with Blair makes so much sense now. Similar to what you alluded to a few weeks ago, she suggested I wait to decide about signing with her until after the merger is over."

"I think that's smart, Sophia. If you need anything in the meantime, you know Blair will help you. I'm always here to support anything you need, too."

"Thanks for that," Sophia says. "I appreciate it. I'm definitely signing with Blair just as soon as she figures out what her next move is."

I'm pretty sure I know what's next for her, so I tell Sophia I need her help with a surprise for Blair.

The view from my father's office looks over Sunset Blvd. and out toward the Hollywood Hills. The smog in the air is thick today, making the houses nestled in the mountain look glazed over and more like push pins on a bulletin board.

I think about how quickly life can change as I wait for him to arrive. Strangely, I'm not nervous. There's almost an excitement pulsing through me at the thought of never having to see this view again.

The door swings open, and my father strides in with his usual commanding presence.

"Wyatt," he says curtly, closing the door behind him. "I assume you have an explanation for your radio silence last night."

I take a deep breath, meeting his steely gaze. "Yes, I'm resigning from the firm," I say, the words leaving my mouth with determined confidence. "I've accepted a position at Hays and Cole."

The silence that follows is suffocating. For a second, I think he didn't hear me, but then his jaw tightens.

"I see," he says, his voice cold and measured. "After everything this family has invested in you, you're just going to walk away?"

"This isn't about walking away." I walk across the room to face him straight on. "It's about pursuing the career I want, making my own decisions."

He takes an intimidating step closer. "This is about chasing that woman."

"Blair has nothing to do with this. This is about me choosing what's right for me."

He raises an eyebrow, a flicker of annoyance crossing his face.

"You think Hays and Cole will tolerate your distractions? Please, I've had to cover for you on more occasions than you even realize. You'll never make it there."

"Look, I appreciate everything you've done. There's no denying that a good part of my success is because of you—"

"Spare me the sentimental drivel. Unfortunately, you can't leave. Your departure will jeopardize the TWA project. You're leading it, and we're too far along to replace you without consequences."

"I've already met with their legal teams and Lance," I interject. "I've passed over everything they'll need. They are a smart team, they'll manage just fine."

"This is a mistake, Wyatt. And mistakes have consequences—not just for you."

A chill runs down my spine. "What does that mean?"

"You crossed the line when you chose personal indulgence over professional duty." He adjusts his cufflinks, his movements deliberate. "And I do what's necessary for the business, Wyatt. You should know that by now."

For a moment, I'm at a loss for words, my heart pounding in my chest. But then it hits me. This is exactly why I'm leaving. I can't be part of this anymore—this manipulation, this power play. I won't let him control my life any longer.

"You do what you have to do. So will I," I say, my voice steady.

"You've always been too emotional, Wyatt. That's your weakness," he sighs, disappointment reflected in his eyes.

"And you've always been self-centered and manipulative," I respond. "That's yours."

His eyes narrow, and for the first time, I see something like uncertainty cross his face. But I don't wait for his response. I turn and walk out of his office, leaving behind everything I've ever known—and finally, life feels like it's starting to make sense.

forty

. . .

BLAIR

I'M HAVING a hard time finding the motivation to walk through the doors of TWA now that I know I won't be here much longer. Plus, I ended up spending the entire weekend at Wyatt's house, and when we weren't naked, he spent hours listening to me get more excited about the possibility of opening my talent management agency.

Lance moved our one-on-one catch-up meeting to today, so I couldn't avoid coming in this morning. Stella meets me at the elevator with a coffee, and while I'm grateful, it's not normal for her to do so.

"I'm suspicious. What's going on?" I ask her.

"Something is up today. I went to see if I could move your meeting with Lance so you could join another meeting, and his assistant refused to flex. Said his schedule was carefully planned out today and he had back-to-back meetings."

My eyes scan the floor as I take a sip of my coffee and look for anything unusual. Most people are here, but it is Monday and after ten o'clock, so that is pretty typical.

"Maybe he's taking off later in the week and is trying to get all of his meetings done before he leaves," I suggest.

"Maybe." She doesn't look convinced.

"I'll see what's up when I meet with him. Did you figure out my schedule with the other thing?"

Stella assures me we're all squared away. Just as I settle in and flip my computer on, Naomi walks in.

"What are you doing here?" I ask her. "I thought you said you were going on vacation?"

Naomi gives me a quick hug and hello. "Meeting with Lance. But the good news is I'm now on permanent vacation." She leans back and kicks her feet up on the chair next to her, and I take that as a cue to get up and shut my office door.

"Stella, I'm going to need a minute with Naomi."

The door closes behind me, and I knock down Naomi's feet and take a seat next to her.

"He just fired you?"

"Oh, hell no. I would totally sue his ass if he did that. No, he informed me that my role has been eliminated to help streamline redundancies and reduce costs. It wasn't a reflection of my work here at TWA and was strictly a business decision, blah, blah, blah. I'm certain he was reading from a script."

"When is your last day?"

"Today? I don't really know, but they are delusional if they think I'm going to continue working here like nothing has happened."

Naomi leans forward and puts her hands on my knees. "He literally said, *I know this is a lot to digest, so feel free to take the rest of the day off.*" She pulls away, laughing like she's heard the best punchline to a joke.

"What is the severance? What about non-compete?" I ask her.

"I'm not sure yet. He read through some high-level info, but HR is supposed to reach out in the next twenty-four hours with specific info. From what I could understand, we'll be allowed to move to any agency, which is nice, but our clients won't necessarily follow us. And I need to confirm the severance. He said I'd be paid out for the remainder of my contract, but mine was expiring at the end of the year. I'm going to need more than a few months' pay for all the years I gave him."

Same here.

"You're well respected in this industry, Naomi. If someone wants to follow you, they will. I'm sure there are others out there who wanted you to be their agent, but maybe TWA turned them off."

"I appreciate that, Blair, but I know how this business works."

Just then, my calendar notification goes off.

"Do you need to go?" Naomi asks.

"I'm supposed to meet with Lance in five minutes."

She's quiet as we both realize what I'm walking into.

"That sucks, babe. I didn't think they would ever let you go."

I don't hear the rest of what she's saying. Everything around me stops, and I'm suddenly nervous. I knew this was happening, but I didn't realize it would be today. Everything

I haven't thought about comes rushing forward as if they are competing for a gold medal.

I haven't given my clients a heads-up.

What if people hear about it from the trades before I can tell them?

What about Stella? Will she be impacted?

I'm surprised at the hurt feelings that surface. I've given my blood, sweat, and tears to this agency, and I'm great at my job. I'm furious that they would just toss me out so easily.

"Can you stay here?" I ask Naomi.

"Sure, hon. I'll be right here."

I walk down the hall and tap on Lance's door.

"Blair! Come on in. How was your weekend?"

This man is unbelievable. If he's really letting me go, he has some nerve with the small talk.

"It was great. What can I do for you?"

"Have a seat. Please."

I sit across from him, with his desk between us. He leans forward, places his elbows on his desk, and clasps his hands in front of him. My eyes dart over every move he makes, trying to read his intentions.

"Blair, I'm just going to cut to the chase. It's no secret the business is struggling. We're still recovering from the pandemic. Movie audiences continue to decline. Streaming services can't figure out how to make money, and the writers' strike didn't help. All of this has impacted TWA's bottom line, too, and there's even more pressure with this merger."

The chase he did not cut to. I just nod and let him continue. Naomi's right. He's definitely reading from a script, but I'm almost positive he's memorized it. Or maybe there's a teleprompter behind my head. It's not out of the realm of possibility—I didn't get a good look around the room before I sat down.

"I'm sorry to tell you, but your position has been eliminated."

"When is this effective?" I ask.

"HR will reach out after this meeting to share all the specifics."

"What about Stella?"

"This decision doesn't impact Stella. In fact, Brian needs a new assistant, so we'll be moving her over to his desk."

I feel relieved that Stella won't lose her job, but I vow to hire her the second I land on my feet again. "Who else knows about this?"

"We're notifying affected employees all day today, and then tomorrow, I will let the office know we had to make some tough decisions. Please hold off on letting your team know any specifics until I've had a chance to send a note."

Lance stands and extends his hand to shake mine. I stand and reach out. "I'll be honest, Blair. I figured Wyatt would have told you everything already. It was his idea to lay off employees with contracts expiring soon."

I can feel my heart beating in my chest, but I don't say a word because I'm not sure what Lance's angle is here. He's fishing for something, though, and I won't take the bait. And he's trying to cause drama by suggesting my fate was at the hands of Wyatt. What I won't share is how Wyatt already admitted that some of his ideas inadvertently put a target on my back. It wasn't intentional. How would he have even known about my contract with TWA?

"Thanks again, Blair. You've always been the consummate professional. It's been a pleasure to work with you. You will be missed."

I'm not sure if it's the shiny joker grin on his face, the amount of contradiction in what he's saying to me, or the sudden relief I feel now that I don't have to work for him anymore, but something in me snaps. Holding my breath, I nod and stride for the door, eager to exit before the laughter threatening to burst forth can escape. It would be highly inappropriate and very unflattering. I'm not a fucking idiot. I know I have to play the part of a professional yet wounded employee until I'm back in the safety of my office.

Stella's confused face causes me to break, and I drag her into my office, where Naomi is waiting. As soon as the door shuts, my shoulders shake with the absurdity of the situation, and I howl with laughter. When Naomi joins in, clutching my arm, I know Stella thinks we've lost our minds.

"It's nothing personal," Naomi snorts out.

"Except you're redundant," I chime in, doing my best Lance impression.

"What is going on?" Stella yells.

That catches both Naomi and me by surprise, and we settle down enough to fill her in on what's happening. I swear her to secrecy since I'm technically not supposed to tell anyone on my team until tomorrow, but there was no way I would have kept this from Stella. I haven't signed any NDAs. I also tell her she's safe but not to get too comfortable because I'm coming for her as soon as I can.

"I'm calling Jess," Stella says as she dials on the speakerphone.

"Oh, now she calls me," Jess spits out once she's on the line. "After going MIA all weekend, she wants to talk."

"You're on speaker. Stella and Naomi are in here, too," I tell her so she knows now isn't the time to talk about my weekend. I should've known an audience would only hype her up more.

"Perfect. Then you'll only have to give the details about banging Wyatt all weekend once!"

"And here I thought you'd want an exclusive for your podcast," I say to force the subject change, and it works.

"Well, fuck. You win. Spill it."

We give Jess the details about the meetings Naomi and I had with Lance this morning, and Stella shares that more have been planned throughout the day. This implies that a few more top leaders are likely being laid off. It's not enough for a full story, but this is Hollywood, and there's nothing more exciting than a social post that starts: *Happening Now* and ends with *Updates Ongoing*.

"I'm hanging up so I can chase this story," Jess says, "but drinks later so we can hear more about Blatt."

"What is Blatt?" Naomi asks.

"We're not doing that," I say.

"It's their ship name! That is so cute!" Stella says.

"It's the worst!" I say.

"It sounds like a bug hitting a windshield," Naomi chimes in.

"You're welcome," Jess says, and then the line cuts out.

Naomi stands, gives Stella and me each a strong, tight hug, and makes a promise to call in a few days once she's finished celebrating her freedom from TWA.

After Naomi leaves, I notice that Stella is still planted in my office. Then I realize that while we were all joking about leaving, she wasn't.

"Hey, you ok?" I ask her. "You know I'm serious about hiring you as soon as I land somewhere. And you know Brian. He's harmless. You'll be just fine."

"Oh, I'm not worried about that. I mean, without a doubt, you better come get me as soon as you can, but I was actually thinking about something else."

She stands and looks like she's going to leave without finishing her thought, but then she surprises me with her next words. "What did it feel like? With Wyatt? The connection you had with him the first time, and is it different now? I just was curious. What made you feel like he was the one for you?"

I think about her question for a minute because it's hard to find words for something as intangible as emotions and intuition. A warm smile spreads across my face as I recount my journey with Wyatt.

"I don't know if I realized it at first. In the beginning, he made me feel understood and cherished. He still does. And that felt different. I'd never experienced those feelings with anyone else before. I've always felt like he sees the best parts of me, even when I can't. And now there's this unshakeable foundation of mutual respect and support. When I'm with him, it's this incredible mix of comfort and excitement, like coming home and embarking on a new adventure all at once."

"And you love him," Stella says. It's not a question.

"I'm completely and madly in love with him."

I realize I want him to know exactly how I feel, too.

forty-one

· · ·

WYATT

AFTER THE CONFRONTATION with my father, I expected backlash, but I never expected him to help Lance and the team accelerate the layoffs so Blair would be affected just a few days later.

The minute she called to tell me the news, I knew it was a silent punch from my father. What he doesn't realize is that the only damage he did was between him and me. Although, I should probably thank him. Nothing like a life change to make you reaffirm your feelings, and in Blair's case, it gave her the courage to take the first step in making our relationship official. When she told me she loved me, it was like I could breathe again—and I didn't even know I was holding my breath.

When Blair and I realized we both had some unexpected free time on our hands, I whisked her away on a quick trip to Palm Springs, where I had the pleasure of watching her walk around with little to no clothing all week. It was divine timing. Our lives were dramatically shifting around us, but at the same time, they were giving us the gift of reconnecting and building something even better—a life together.

Now that we're back in LA and I've officially started at Hays and Cole, I've enlisted some help to show Blair how serious I am about our future. Sophia, along with Jess and Stella, is taking her to lunch, and I'll meet up with them this afternoon.

As Jake saunters into my office, I can't help but smile.

"Well, this is new. Happier than I've ever seen you. I suppose it's about time."

"You're right, Jake. I've never felt this happy. Standing up to my father and starting at Hays and Cole—it's like a weight has been lifted off my shoulders. And the best part? I got the girl."

Jake grins and leans against the door frame. "It's been a journey, that's for sure. Speaking of Blair, the paperwork is all in order. I must say, you've really gone all out for this surprise. I'm happy for you, man."

"Thanks again for all your help with this. I can't wait to see the look on her face."

Just then, my phone buzzes with a text. It's Sophia.

"Hey, check this out," I say, showing Jake my phone. "Sophia wants to surprise Blair too. She wants to sign with Blair and wants me to draft a preliminary contract. She wants it ready so Blair can see it right away."

Jake whistles. "That's huge."

I nod, already mentally drafting the contract in my head. "I just want everything to be perfect for Blair. Her friends are distracting her until the afternoon. When they bring her to the office space, I'll be there to surprise her."

Jake claps me on the shoulder. "Congrats, Wyatt. You deserve this happiness."

"Thanks, Jake. For everything. I wouldn't be here today if it weren't for you."

We hug it out, and I get back to completing the details for this afternoon. What I haven't shared with anyone else is that I'm also going to ask Blair to move in with me. I know it's fast, but we've wasted too much time already, and I don't want to spend another day without her. I'd propose right now, too, but one step at a time.

———

That afternoon, I'm standing in the empty office space, and my heart pounds with anticipation. The room is bathed in the soft afternoon light, casting a warm glow on the polished wooden floors. I've set up a few essentials: a sleek, modern desk with a comfortable chair for Blair and a receptionist desk near the entrance. Everything is ready.

As I hear footsteps approaching, my pulse quickens. Blair's friends have done a great job of keeping her occupied until now. The door swings open, and there she is, her eyes widening in surprise as she takes in the room.

"Wyatt, what's going on?" she asks, a mix of confusion and curiosity in her voice.

"Blair, I know how much you've dreamed of having your own talent management agency. This space is leased for the next year, just for you."

I step forward, holding out an envelope. Her hands tremble slightly as she takes it and opens it to reveal the paperwork inside. Tears fill her eyes as she reads, and her gaze darts back to me.

"You did this for me?" she whispers, her voice choked with emotion.

I nod, stepping closer. "You deserve it, Blair. You've worked so hard, and I believe in you. This is your chance to create something amazing."

She looks around the office, her eyes lingering on the new furniture. "It's perfect," she says, her voice filled with awe. "I can't believe you did this."

I take her hand and squeeze it gently. "I wanted to give you a place where you can build your dreams. You inspire me every day, and I want to support you in every way I can."

Blair throws her arms around me and pulls me into a tight embrace. "Thank you, Wyatt. This means everything to me."

"Ok, ok, you two love each other," Jess says. "We get it." I'll never call her out on it, but I swear I see her blinking away tears. She comes over to congratulate Blair and then gives me a pat on the arm.

"Good job boyfriend," Jess whispers.

I can't help the smile that stretches over my face.

"Ok, we're not done," I tell everyone as I nod to Sophia. "There's one more surprise."

She pulls out another envelope and hands it to Blair. "I'd like to be your first client, if you still want me."

The look on Blair's face is worth all the drama and hurdles we had to fight through to get here. She pulls Sophia into a hug, and they jump around like a couple of kids instead of the Oscar-winning actress and top executive they are.

"You're a good man, Wyatt Bradford," says Jess. "Take care of our girl."

"You guys act like I'm being shipped off somewhere," says Blair. "I'm right here."

"Yeah, but you're his now," Stella chimes in. "This is where the torch gets passed, and he's your person."

"Yeah, I guess he is." Blair curls into my side and wraps her arm around my waist. "Hope you know what you're getting into."

forty-two

. . .

WYATT

I GUESS when you live with a guest to Grant's end-of-summer bash, you get to be a plus-one. Automatic invite. That's the only reason I agreed to travel to the Hamptons for Labor Day weekend. It is absolutely the worst time to be there.

When I walk into our beach rental, I don't expect to see Blair standing in the living room. She is perfection. She's wearing a deep red dress that hugs every single curve on her body. The straps wrap around her neck and split down the center, showcasing her spectacular tits. The hemline is long, but it has a slit up her right leg, hitting her at mid-thigh. She's swept the top half of her hair off her face and into a ponytail to join the rest of the thick waves cascading down her back. I'm both speechless and immediately possessive. Her darkened, smoky eyes give her a dramatic look, and her lips match the red of her dress. Immediately, I want to see those lips around my dick and the stain she would leave behind.

"You look incredible."

"So do you, Mr. Bradford." Blair wraps her arms around my neck, careful with her kiss so she doesn't ruin her makeup.

I'm wearing a dark gray Dior suit with a navy shirt underneath. I bought the outfit special so I could make a good impression on this Hamptons crowd. I don't want this to be my last invite, so I dressed to impress.

"Where's Sophia?" I ask.

"With Brandon. Upstairs. We're not alone, so you can stop thinking about how you're going to get into this dress before the party."

"I'm sure I can find a way," I wink. "Let's go up. I want to thank Brandon for letting us crash here."

I reach out to pinch her side and then follow her upstairs where Brandon is relaxing on a sofa in the loft area. "Hey man, thanks again for letting us stay here. This house is incredible." He rises and grabs my hand to pull me in for a bro hug. "Anytime man. So glad you could make it. Soph is in there." He gestures toward double doors partially open.

Sophia's room looks like the closet and bathroom exploded. I look around, and just then, my sister exits the bathroom, looking like she's ready to accept her next Oscar.

"You look like fucking Cinderella! Wow, Soph!" I walk over to kiss her on the cheek, but she pulls back immediately.

"Don't mess up my face!" she squeals. "Thank you, though. You look very Prince Charming yourself. Nice suit."

I look over at Blair as she laughs with Brandon, and I can see my entire future with her. This is us getting ready for premieres and openings. I'm with her at every event. I wake up with her in my arms and fall asleep every night with her by my side.

"Just get a ring, already," Sophia says.

"Calm down," I reply. "We just moved in together."

Sophia shakes her head like she already knows it's going to happen any moment now and it's a waste of time trying to convince her otherwise.

"Let's go, people!" she shouts. "Time to party!" My sister is way too excited about this end-of-summer party.

When we get to Grant's house, we're escorted outside, and I'm impressed by what I see.

A long dinner table stretches in front of us, covered in white linens and tall white candles. Surrounding the table in a tent-like shape are thousands of strands of tiny white lights, giving the patio a look of glamour and magic.

We walk under the lights and find our seats among the other guests. We're near the head of the table, with Sophia placed to the right of Grant, who's seated at the top.

A Michelin chef caters the twelve-course tasting menu, featuring a tour of Japanese culture. The menu looks incredible, and I'm eager to try the fatty tuna belly topped with caviar and the smoked scallop with wasabi.

As we wait to be served, Grant addresses the crowd. "Every year, I vow to skip the speech and spare everyone the pain of listening to my nostalgic memories from past dinners. This year is no different, but once again, I find myself inspired by you." He glances at Sophia.

Blair looks at me with eyes that say, *Did you see that?*

I did.

"This town has no shortage of talent and inspiration,

but finding the right mix of creativity, humanity, and connection is rare. Some of you have never attended this celebration before, and some have been coming since I started this tradition ten years ago. If you are here, you are important to me. You are what I consider the best of the best. Many people in this town joke that the best relationship in Hollywood is no relationship. But I've found that I've had my best days when I'm surrounded and supported by all of you. I'm grateful for your friendship. Cheers to you."

We all raise our glasses to toast the moment.

Blair glances at me again and mouths with a smirk, *We are important to Grant.* I don't doubt that most people here are—this is a super exclusive invite.

"Why do you think we are really here?" I whisper close to her ear.

"Your sister."

I take a deep breath because it gives me heartburn that he's so much older than her.

"She doesn't date. Someone should tell him he doesn't have a chance."

"It looks like she might reconsider her no-dating rule."

Sophia and Grant huddle close, smiling and laughing with one another. Inside, guests are sipping champagne and talking to one another. This is why you want to be at this party. It's a free pass to talk shop, get intimate with the elite in this business, and make great connections and impressions. While I want to take advantage of this opportunity, I want Blair more.

"I'm going to run to the bathroom," Blair says.

"Want me to go with you?" I wink at her, and she winks back.

"Maybe."

She holds my stare as she walks away, and I'm not going to question it. I follow her a minute later.

When I step into the only bathroom at the top of the stairs, I find her waiting for me, leaning against the sink. I press into her body, letting her feel all of me. Then I raise my hand to grasp her jaw and crash my lips against hers.

"I barely made it through dinner. I've been thinking about being inside you since I saw you in that dress. Turn around."

I help her twist around so her back is against my chest. Then I reach down to her legs and drag my hands up her thighs, sneaking them under her dress.

"This is going to be fast and hard. Are you ready for me, Blair?"

"Yes."

"Bend over and place your hands on the counter."

I unzip my pants and pull them down just enough to reach in and stroke my already hard dick. Thank God we had the talk about protection and I don't need a condom. I can't wait. She looks back at me, and I lean over to kiss her as I push into her dripping-wet pussy.

"Jesus, Blair. You feel so fucking good."

I lean back up and place my hands on her hips to hold her steady as I frantically penetrate her. She's already pulsing around me, and my spine tingles. I reach around to press on her clit so she'll get there faster.

She pushes my hand away so she can play with herself, and I almost blow right then.

"Fuck me harder, Wyatt. I'm so close."

My hips slap against the back of her thighs. I can't get enough, and each thrust feels deeper. I'm so close.

"Wyatt. I'm... Oh, God."

I see stars behind my eyes and I feel her give in to her release.

I pull her up close to me and push into her a few more times before I find my own.

"You are mine." I kiss down the side of her neck before I turn her head and kiss her gently on the lips. "I'll never get enough of you."

We take a minute to put ourselves back together and head back out to the party, hoping nobody has realized we were missing. My arms stay around Blair's body as we head outside, and I pull her onto the makeshift dance floor and sway with her to the music. It's a perfect evening.

"Hey, beautiful."

"Hey, handsome."

I pull her close and nuzzle my face into the side of her neck. "This has been a pretty great summer," I whisper.

"It has," she says, "but I'm not sure the version of me in May would believe it if I told her how this summer would end."

"How long do you think we need to stay so we get an invite for next year?" I ask Blair.

"I think we've stayed an appropriate amount of time."

I take her hand, and we head back to the bar area to find Sophia. She's there, standing next to Jake.

"Hey, you made it!" I say. "I'm so glad you came."

"Lauren is missing out. I can't believe she couldn't make it," Blair says as she wraps her arm around my waist and leans in for a quick kiss.

"Her trip to Mexico was planned before we knew about this. Maybe she can make it next year." Jake's face shifts into a look of frustration and sadness and then back to his default happiness so quickly that I would've missed it if I didn't know him so well. I'll have to ask him if everything is ok when we're back in the office next week.

"Definitely next year." I give him a supportive smile.

"So, I think we're going to head out," Blair says. "You ready, Soph?"

"I think I'll hang for a little longer. I can grab a car to bring me back."

We say a quick goodbye to Jake and a few others before we sneak out undetected by our host and then start the drive back to the beach house.

"Is it weird that Jake and Lauren just got back from their honeymoon and she's already taking a trip to Mexico with her girlfriends?" Blair asks.

"Definitely weird," I tell her, "especially since she cut the honeymoon short."

"Please promise me you'll never cut our honeymoon short."

I don't even think Blair realizes what she's said.

"I promise," I reply. "I'm just happy to hear there's a honeymoon in our future."

She drops her head into my chest, embarrassed by what she's said, but I pull her chin up so she's looking up at me.

"I'd marry you tomorrow if you'd let me, Blair."

"Let's make it through another season, and then we can talk," she jokes.

I kiss her gently and then more intentionally, letting her know I plan to hold her to that timeline. She leans against me, resting her head on my chest, and I let my mind wander to the holiday season and what a proposal might look like. I make a mental note to go ring shopping when I'm back in LA. Then I pull Blair closer and kiss the top of her head, knowing I have so much to look forward to.

epilogue

. . .

SIX MONTHS LATER

blair

"THIS HAS BEEN QUITE a year so far, Ms. Bennett," Wyatt whispers in my ear as we look out at the crowd of friends and family here to celebrate today. When Wyatt leased this office space for me, I wasn't sure how fast I would be able to open.

"And it's only just beginning," I say.

Wyatt helped me negotiate a more lucrative severance package from TWA, leveraging the fallout of Lance's indiscretions at the office. Turns out Naomi and her assistant weren't his only flings. He slept with two junior agents from the TV division, but the nail in the coffin was getting caught in a compromising position in the storage closet with his assistant. He unraveled so spectacularly that both Wyatt and Jake were able to influence him to agree to honor the severance policy or contract in place, whichever is longer, in exchange for their help in negotiating his own exit package.

The severance, along with some savings, meant I could open my agency faster than expected. I convinced Naomi and Stella to join me, and we signed Sophia, Edie, and a few others. Today, we're finally putting up the sign on the small building Wyatt leased for me a few months ago. Tangerine Talent is official.

Wyatt and Stella co-conspired to make this a bigger-than-expected celebration with some of our friends, causing me to pretend I had dust in my eye and not actually crying. I'll never get used to how much Wyatt celebrates and cheers me on.

"I can't believe you put all this together," I tell him. "It's thoughtful and sweet, and you're definitely getting lucky tonight."

"I can't take all the credit. Stella did a lot of the work, but I'm sure she won't object if you show me how much you appreciate all she's done, too."

Wyatt scans my face like he's trying to memorize every feature. Then he holds me close with his arms wrapped around my waist. I want to freeze these moments. Being in his arms makes me feel wanted and loved.

I moved in with Wyatt just before Grant's end-of-summer bash in the Hamptons. It was fast, but we both knew it would happen eventually, so why delay the inevitable? I still have my house, and we're renting it to Stella's friend Natalie. She just wrote her first screenplay. Maybe one day, she'll be part of the Tangerine family.

We finally sold Edie's project to Grant, and the surprise twist is that Sophia will help produce and star in the film. Pre-production has just started, and it's been a blast to see it coming to life. I notice Grant has been part of every meeting, too, and I can't decide if it's because she's a young new producer or a young, beautiful, single woman.

Speak of the devil.

"Blair, you've totally transformed this space. It looks amazing. Congratulations!" Sophia kisses both my cheeks and squeezes me so tightly that I lose my breath for a minute.

"Congrats, Blair," Grant says once Sophia releases me, sliding in for a half-hug and a quick peck on my cheek. "This was a long time coming. I'm looking forward to watching you change this business."

"Thanks, you two. And thanks for being my very first project under the Tangerine banner. I'm so excited to be working with you both!"

"Hey, Soph. Hey, Grant." Wyatt embraces his sister and shakes Grant's hand. He and Grant have been spending more time together, building their bromance, and Grant even made the invite to Manmorial weekend this year. I think Wyatt softened a bit when he saw Grant out of the Hollywood exec context and spending time with his daughter, Hazel.

Stella walks up. "Hey, Blair. I don't mean to interrupt, but if you want to say a few words first, I'll start passing out the cake and champagne after."

I excuse myself and head to the back to take a moment for myself. Some days, it's surreal to think that I can do what I love and get paid for it. I look around the room, and my heart fills with gratitude for the people in this town who have become my family.

"You ready?" Jess brushes my hair off my shoulders and

rests her arms around my neck. "I brought Porto's. You can't open this agency without our favorite food!"

I laugh and hug her. I love this woman.

"Get out there, lady. Time to be a boss bitch!"

I squeeze her hand and then head to the front door. Wyatt notices me walking and clanks his glass with his fork to get everyone's attention.

"Ok, ok. This isn't that formal of an event," I say, looking around the room with a smile stretched wide across my face. "Every single person here means so much to me. You've changed my life for the better, and more importantly, I wouldn't want to know a life without you. When I became an agent, I saw a shift happening in Hollywood and with women. We were starting to demand more. It was exciting. I was lucky to find an agency that let me build my experience exploring projects where I could place women and convince studios to take a chance.

"But the past few years, it's felt like mainstream Hollywood has been in a panic and reverting to the old ways, ways that are comfortable and don't challenge the status quo. I've dreamed about building a place where I could focus on representing female talent who are dedicated to their craft, particular about roles and writing, and looking to truly shape the culture of our industry. Talent who are after roles that will ultimately help change our world for the better. I know it's a lofty thought here in Hollywood."

I look out at the crowd and see nods and smiles, encouragement for my dream.

"Thank you, Sophia and Edie, for taking a chance on me. Tangerine is so proud to represent such talented, fierce women. And thanks to the rest of you. I won't name names because I know I'll leave someone out. Your support and belief in me inspires me daily.

"And to Wyatt. I am overwhelmed with gratitude for the unwavering love and support you have shown me. Your encouragement, patience, and belief in my dreams have given me the courage to pursue this venture. Thank you for the late-night brainstorming sessions and the tough love when I needed it. There's nobody else I'd want by my side for this journey ahead."

I can't hide my glistening eyes. Thankfully, I see a few others with the same shine.

"To me, the tangerine symbolizes more than just luck and prosperity; it represents creativity, vitality, and the sweetness of success after hard work. I named my agency Tangerine Talent to capture that spirit of optimism and to celebrate the vibrant journey of every artist we represent. Please join me in a toast to celebrate Tangerine Talent and the bright futures we're nurturing together!"

The clinking of glasses echoes as chatter fills the room. I walk over to Wyatt, who's standing against the wall with his hands in his pockets. He's got a smirk on his face that says he's feeling pretty happy about that public declaration I just made.

"Hey," I say.

"Nice speech."

"Thanks."

We stare at each other for a minute, and then he pushes off the wall and wraps an arm around my waist.

"I'm in such awe of you. I love how you push people to

reach beyond the status quo, and I love the stories you are pushing out into the world. You inspire so many women, and you inspire me. Congratulations, Blair. You deserve every bit of this."

I look around the room to take in the moment.

I wouldn't change a thing.

wyatt

I'm nervous and excited as Blair and I pull into our driveway. The past six months of living together have been everything I imagined. Even though it was fast, we fell right into a comfortable and easy routine. The feelings we had all those years ago still burn today. Of course, some days are spicier than others, and we're learning how to navigate the few times we don't agree on things, but our love for each other runs deep and is all-consuming.

I want to marry her as soon as possible. I want her to have my name—and my babies if she wants them. I can't wait until she is fully mine and there is no question that she belongs with me, in our home, at my side, for every adventure.

I've hidden a blanket and bottle of champagne on my back patio. The plan is to convince her to have a nightcap with me on the beach to toast our successful year. Then I can surprise her with another reason to raise our glasses.

"Let's go out back for a minute," I say to her. "It's such a beautiful night."

I lead her to the back doors, and as she walks out, I

quickly open the drawer on the end table by the couch and grab the ring I hid earlier today.

"I'll never tire of coming out here," she says. "It's so beautiful."

"It is." But I'm not looking at the beach; I'm looking at her. She turns, sees me staring at her, and comes back to kiss me.

I break the kiss and grab her hand. "Come on. I think there's some champagne over here. Let's go have a glass while we sit in the sand for a minute."

"You just happen to have champagne out here?" Blair asks, looking around with a confused frown while I pull her onto the beach. I do my best to deflect the question and stick to the plan.

I lay the blanket on the soft sand and motion for her to sit. Then I open the champagne and hand her a glass.

"So, what should we toast to?" she asks.

"Us," I tell her.

It's now or never. "When I lost you that summer—when I left you—I left my heart with you. I didn't take it with me. I didn't give it to anyone else, and I didn't think I would use it ever again. I can't take back what I did or give us back the time we lost, but I can promise you I'll never lose another moment with you. I'm yours."

I dip my forehead to touch hers.

"Wyatt, I'm yours, too. I always have been."

I grab her glass of champagne and set it with mine off to the side. Then I pull the small box from my pocket and open it for her to see. Hopefully, the look of shock on her face is a positive sign.

"I can't imagine a future that doesn't have you by my side, and I don't want to. The thought of spending the rest of my life with you, building a life together, fills me with more joy than I ever thought possible. I want to be there for you, to support you, to laugh with you, and to love you in every way I can. Will you marry me, Blair?"

Before the question leaves my mouth, Blair rushes to hug me, and her excitement forces us to tumble over on the blanket. I fall flat on my back, with her resting on top of me.

She covers my mouth with her lips while saying, "Yes, yes, yes," and then peppers my face with tiny kisses as she continues to say, "Yes," over and over.

"I'll take that as a yes." I laugh and roll us back up so I can put the ring on her finger.

Blair holds her hand out to admire the ring. She didn't even look at it before tackling me, and I'm afraid I may go down again once she has a peek. It's a two-carat princess cut diamond on a platinum band, with two one-carat princess cut diamonds on each side, representing our past, the present, and the future to come.

The tears well up in her eyes, and I swipe my thumb across her cheek to catch them as they begin to drop.

"Happy tears, I hope?" I ask.

"This ring. It's so gorgeous. It's perfect."

I hand over her glass of champagne and raise mine for a toast.

"To Mr. and Mrs. Bradford." I pause for a minute and look at her. "You don't have to change your name."

"I can't wait to be Mrs. Bradford."

We sip our champagne, but before we finish, Blair stands.

"Let's go inside, Mr. Bradford. I'd like to practice for our wedding night, husband."

"Anything you want, wife." I lean forward to kiss her and then give her a wink as I say, "Maybe we can leave only the heels on tonight."

I know there will never be a better feeling than this. She's my one and only. She always has been.

more from the author

Not ready for the love story to end?

Get a bonus scene and other updates when you Scan the QR code
to sign up for my newsletter.

The Backlot Series

Second Act – Available Now!

Center Stage – coming April 2025

(Sophia and Grant's story)

Coming in 2025 and 2026

On the Record

Behind the Scenes

Off Script

Thank you!

I hope you loved *Second Act*! If you did, leaving a review would mean so much—it helps other readers discover the story and makes a huge difference for indie authors like me!

acknowledgments

Well, here we are! This book is finally in your hands, and I'm beyond grateful to everyone who made it possible.

First things first... family.

To my incredible daughter: thank you for being one of my first sounding boards for plot ideas and character developments. Your patience and support, especially when I disappeared into my writing cave, meant the world to me. Blair's confidence and passion are 100% inspired by you! I love you more than words can say, and I'm so proud to be your mom.

To my mom: You've always believed in me and been my biggest fan. Thank you for being the first in line for everything I've ever done—whether reading, watching, or cheering me on. I love you so much, and I'm so lucky to have you in my corner.

To my sisters, Kristy and Jamie: You are the funniest people I know, and life with you has been one hilarious adventure after another. Your blind loyalty is unmatched—whether I'm right or wrong, you're there cheering me on, no questions asked. I love you both so much, and I'm so glad we get to do life together. Big thanks to your guys for lending me their names, too!

And then... friends.

Cami and Holly, my besties: What would I do without

you? Holly, you've known me since we were teens and can verify all the "truths" hidden in this book. Cami, you're my emotional support system—there for me day in and day out, lifting me up when I need it most. Both of you listened to my endless ramblings about these characters when you probably had better things to do. You're two of the most supportive, incredible humans I know and I love you both endlessly.

My entertainment crew—Carol, Erin, Monica, Rachelle, Chris, Rob, Jennifer, Jenn: Thank you for the plot discussions, PR coaching, fact-checking, and all the support. We really did work at the best company ever once upon a time.

Can't forget... the professionals.

Thank you to those who helped shape and support this book: Jessica at HEA Author Services—your feedback made this into a real story; Jefferson at First Editing—your advice made the tension stronger; Stacy at Quirky Bird—your cover design is incredible, and your indie author advice was a game-changer; Taylor at Tag Media Agency—your digital marketing expertise helped make me visible to the world; Ellie at Love Notes PR—thank you for bringing my words to the fans!

To my beta readers: Your feedback refined my characters and dialogue, making the emotions hit just right. This book is so much better because of you.

To my ARC readers: I'm so excited to meet you and thank you so much for taking a chance on this newbie author. I look forward to getting to know all of you better and appreciate being part of your community!

Finally, to the indie authors, BookTokers, and readers who have followed and cheered me on—I'm thrilled to be part of this community with you. Special shoutout to the queens who paved the way and inspired my ambition: Melanie Harlow, Elle Kennedy, Laura Pavlov, Meghan Quinn, Elsie Silver, and Kandi Steiner. I hope to one day write stories as memorable as yours.

And to anyone who takes a chance on me and reading my words - thank you for being a part of making my dreams come true. Your support means the world to me!

about the author

Kimberly Page is a contemporary romance author who loves writing about strong heroines and the irresistible heroes who fall for them. After a career spent crafting stories for major players in the entertainment industry, she decided to create stories of her own.

When she's not writing, you can find Kimberly planning for beach time, at a theme park with her daughter, or getting lost in a good sports romance book. Follow her on TikTok and Instagram for news and updates.

www.kimberlyjpage.com